Patience, My Dear

A NOVEL

Arianna Snow

Golden Horse Ltd.
Cedar Rapids, Iowa

An *Original Publication of Golden Horse Ltd.*
P.O. Box 1002
Cedar Rapids, IA 52406-1002 U.S.A.
www.ariannaghnovels.com

ISBN: 0-9772308-0-5

Library of Congress Control Number: 2005932840

Printed and bound in the United States of America by Publisher's Graphics, LLC

Cover: Design by Arianna Snow
        Photography by Rachael McClenahan
        Layout by CEZ
        Printed by White Oak Printing

Dedicated with love and gratitude to:

God, for inspiring me to author this book

my husband, with whom I found true love

Desilama Raheleka:
my children, their significant others, my grandbabies —
the residents of my heart and spirit

my loving parents M & J ,
who have faith in my creative endeavors

my brothers J. R. & R. and their families,
for their support

Dear LB, MH,
friends and relatives around the world

my wonderful phone sisters
RC PJ LV

my cherished pets

THOSE OF SCOTTISH DESCENT

♥ my love and special thanks

to

KAE, LC RE and HR

for their time and patience

with

edititorial assistance and marketing ♥

It was August of nineteen hundred and thirteen, in Lochmoor Glen, Scotland. In exactly twelve months, the residents of this quaint village would join millions around the globe, to face the devastation and loss of loved ones in the First World War. Until then, the populace, continued in the trials, triumphs, and tribulations of everyday relationships.

This is an account of a British couple, reunited with the peril of their inflamed past. The man, a faithless recluse, confronts life in the outside world. The woman struggles to maintain a desirable balance between her search for human love and her spiritual devotion. Their intertwined lives integrated, with the common variables of time, place, and new relationships, produce an unpredictable future.

HIRAM GEOFFREY MCDONNALLY FAMILY TREE

PATERNAL GRANDPARENTS;

CAPTAIN GEOFFREY EDWARD MCDONNALLY

CATHERINE NORTON MCDONNALLY

FATHER;

CAPTAIN GEOFFREY LACHLAN MCDONNALLY

UNCLE

EDWARD CALEB MCDONNALLY

MATERNAL GRANDPARENTS;

ALEXANDER THOMAS SELRACH

SARAH GLASGOW SELRACH

MOTHER;

AMANDA SELRACH MCDONNALLY

NAOMI BEATRICE (MACKENZIE) MCDONNALLY FAMILY TREE

PATERNAL GRANDPARENTS

JEREMIAH NORMAN MACKENZIE

OCTAVIA HILL MACKENZIE

FATHER

NATHAN ELIAS MACKENZIE

MATERNAL GRANDPARENTS

JAMES HENRY SMITHFIELD

IRENE CLEBOURNE SMITHFIELD

MOTHER;

BEATRICE SMITHFIELD MACKENZIE

BROTHER

JEREMIAH JAMES MACKENZIE

STEPMOTHER:

DAGMAR ARNOLDSON MACKENZIE

The Chapters

I   *Hiram*

II   *The Encounter*

III   *The Truth*

IV   *The Voice*

V   *The Woods*

VI   *The Avenger*

VII   *The Guest*

VIII   *The Picnic*

IX   *Duncan Ridge*

X   *The Secret*

XI   *Heidi*

XII   *The Visit*

Chapter 1

"Hiram"

"In the swamp in secluded recesses,
A shy and hidden bird is warbling a song.
Solitary the thrush,
The hermit withdrawn to himself, avoiding the settlements,
Sings by himself a song."

—Walt Whitman

The haunting, amber glow of two eyes penetrated the inescapable darkness of the moors, as the barely visible motorcar prowled cautiously up the knoll on that sultry, summer evening. It came to rest in a deserted cobblestone drive, beneath four alabaster columns, of a seemingly abandoned, but not forgotten mansion, known as Lochmoor's McDonnally Manor. Not so long ago, well-groomed equestrian teams, escorting the finest carriages on the British Isles, waited patiently here for the regal elite to return from countless galas.

A single passenger stepped out, glared at the mansion's crumbling façade, reluctantly closed the door, and then remorsefully watched the vehicle disappear into the misty hillside, as leisurely as it had arrived. The large-framed man navigated quietly through the moonlight, toward the portal, dodging the tall thistles growing between the stones. Hiram Geoffrey McDonnally hesitated slightly, drew a deep breath, and nervously retrieved the familiar key from the pocket of his grey plaid waistcoat, beneath his tweed jacket. He turned the key slowly and unlocked the door, behind which an array of memories was waiting to receive him. Eighteen years had past since he last entered through this door.

His large fingers trembled slightly, yet deftly lifted a match from the corroded tin box on the wall shelf, next to the sidelight. He instinctively lit the oil lamp that hung from the foyer ceiling. The dim flame instantly revealed the familiar massiveness of the corridor and a variety of remnants of his youth; comforting ties to a past life, temporarily forgotten on his journey from the Alps.

With a glimpse at the hammered brass relic in the near corner he thought, *There's the "Indian"* (as his Mother, Amanda, referred to it) *umbrella stand.* Hiram shook his head with disapproval; *Grandfather Selrach would have boiled Margaret in oil, had he seen it in this tarnished condition. Poor Maggie, best of the lot, as maids go, took the blame, willingly, for every mishap in the household.* He recalled that sweet Margaret, never once, denied him permission to use the stand to house his toads, despite his mother's suspicions.

He paused at the gold leaf mirror with apparent discomfort, noticing that time had taken its toll on his once youthful profile. He unconsciously mimicked his father's every movement, silently smoothing his dark trimmed beard and mustache then removed the navy blue watch cap and hung it on the burled oak rack. He ran his fingers through his unruly black curls recalling his father's favorite adage.

"Ah, yes, home is where you hang your hat," his voice echoed sarcastically; for home, it was not. A cloud of dark tumultuous feelings enshrouded him as he turned and his coal-black eyes darted from the winding staircase, to the far corner, where the ominous grandfather clock hovered silently, beside the antique secretary. The smug motionless face of the timepiece beckoned him to come closer.

Conflicting recollections flooded his thoughts. It was an exciting milestone for Hiram, that December day, when his uncle, Edward, seven years his senior, proudly passed the torch giving him, the duty of pulling the weights on the towering clock. He was six years old then, on holiday to the manor, from his grandparents' home in London, where he and Edward had grown up together. There the boys had attended school under the auspices of Hiram's grandmother, Edward's mother, Catherine Norton McDonnally, a slender, red-haired, well-educated woman. During this time in London, Edward naturally took an older brother role model as Hiram's mentor, riding companion, and confidant.

Several years later, with the unexpected passing of Hiram's parents, Edward was given the responsibility as executor of the McDonnally estate. He became temporary Master of McDonnally Manor and assigned guardian to Hiram, the fourteen-year-old heir. The once loving relationship soon became strained with Edward's new authoritative position. It deteriorated further with Hiram's introduction to Naomi MacKenzie, the sweet girl from Newcastle, whom he had met one autumn afternoon at the village market. As time progressed, Hiram became increasingly fond of his female companion, a mere year younger than he, and spent as much time with her as he could afford, denying his uncle, Edward, any knowledge of the relationship. Hiram thrived on his independence coupled with the mystery and the confidentiality surrounding his newfound friendship. Conveniently, Naomi resided with her father and younger brother at Grimwald, an estate sharing the McDonnally property line.

However, in time, the uncle's aroused suspicions inevitably led him to uncover his nephew's secret. Edward adamantly objected to the relationship, believing that the unscrupulous girl, progeny of the unsavory MacKenzie clan, had been solely involved to reap the benefits of Hiram's future position as Master of McDonnally Manor; thus he insisted that his nephew distance himself from the devious young girl. Despite his guardian's demands, and unimpeded by the close proximity of the properties, the enamored young Hiram joined Naomi for afternoon outings, when he was supposedly exercising the horses. Likewise, he continued to meet with her in the wee hours of the morning after his uncle had retired.

Countless mornings, the clock stood as an old soldier that guarded the bleak hall at McDonnally Manor, chiming with the signal that it was "too late" and warning Hiram of his uncle's ensuing wrath for his tardiness. Hiram was only seventeen, when he had last paid homage to the old clock. It had been in that final hour, in his panic to escape up the back staircase, that his cleverness to return unnoticed had betrayed him. On that fateful morning, his adversary was perched on the top step, concealed in a blanket of darkness, like a hawk anticipating its attack on the next available prey.

The once, doting, attentive uncle became obsessively irrational with his young ward's stealthy misconduct, and mercilessly banished Hiram from the mansion for direct insubordination of his wishes to dissolve the relationship with Naomi. With youthful insolence and confusion, perpetuatted by his uncle's stringent measures, young Hiram, rightful heir to McDonnally Manor, vanished with obscuring anger and little more than the shirt on his back, sacrificing his only means of providing a future home for the lovely girl of sixteen.

Hiram thoughts returned from the past, to the clock, as he examined the design and construction for the first time. He had repaired dozens of Swiss clocks similar to this one. Unfortunately, the hours he had spent, engrossed in their workings, had served as a masochistic, daily reminder of the episodes with this grandfather clock and his inability to turn back the hands of time.

"Fourteen past two?" Hiram murmured, as they stood face to face, his stern gaze fixed on the intricately painted hands.

"Was it morning or afternoon when you resigned from your duties?" he questioned rhetorically. They had shared many anxious mornings, in contrast to the cherished afternoons that he had spent with Miss MacKenzie. A wistful smile appeared, as he recounted a particular afternoon, nearly two decades ago, when he had run hand-in-hand through the heather with the fair-skinned, green-eyed girl with flowing auburn hair. Disturbing thoughts of his uncle's intolerance and portraits of star-crossed lovers crept back into the annals of his mind. Even today, eons later, Hiram remained an angry, embittered cynic deprived of the life with his true love.

Agitated, he turned away quickly from the clock and the painful memories, and began desperately searching for anything, that would secure peace to his wounded heart. He passed through the archway, into the parlor, where the heavily draped windows donned cobwebs that filtered the August starlight. The pieces of furniture, cloaked as white specters, seemed to be watching his every move. The stone fireplace was cold and empty, unchanged since "The Banishment."

He glanced down at the thick Persian carpet beneath his boots; Geoffrey McDonnally, his father, had the beautiful rug imported, as a special surprise for his mother, Amanda, a refined woman with Hiram's coloring and black tresses. Despite his frugality, Hiram's father had made every effort to appease his wife's affinity for grandeur to which she had been accustomed to as the magistrate's daughter. More importantly, he had hoped to bring a moment of joy into her apparent melancholy existence.

Mother seldom seemed to be genuinely content. Father claimed that a young man with my "exuberance" would be much happier in London with Grandmother, at least, until mother felt better. She never did. Hiram dubiously considered his father's decision, having been deprived of his mother's presence during his formative years.

Hiram's fondest recollection of his parents was of them embracing encompassed in the archway. Then a vision of his mother, beaming gratefully for the plush floor covering, appeared briefly. Thoughts of that joyful family reunion vanished quickly, with the encroaching memory of his father's premature deployment to Africa with the British troops, splitting the McDonnally unit, once again.

Hiram stood alone in the parlor, just as he did a fortnight after his father left, on the eve of his mother's unanticipated passing, from a contracted bout with influenza. A shroud of despondency fell over him as he studied the portrait of his father positioned above the mantle.

"Captain Geoffrey Lachlan McDonnally, the dignified soldier..." Hiram announced proudly with a hint of skepticism. His father gazed prominently down at him with discernible nobility. Even his father's middle name bore the integrity of the honored Lachlan Macquarie, Hiram's great-great-grandfather's commanding officer, who later became the governor of New South Wales.

When Hiram was two years old, his father had fought proudly in the Zulu War, but during the massacre at Isandhlwana, lost his dearest and oldest friend, Hiram's namesake, Hiram Shalenski. Fortunately, the war ended quickly, allowing Geoffrey to return to his family within the year, but as a changed man. Upon his return, he had few words, in regard to the conflict, with no mention of the spoils of war or the loss of his comrades. Instead, he expounded on his stay in London, which had been assigned its first phone exchange and the "remarkable" availability of frozen Australian meat there. In the years to come, when the topic of the Zulu War surfaced, the Captain defensively began his spiel on the collapse of Scotland's Tay Bridge, which occurred that same year, repeatedly reminding his audience that he had known someone, who had known someone, related to the architect.

Why did he continue in the service? Hiram questioned. Had he chosen not to, Geoffrey may have had the opportunity to say a final goodbye to Hiram's mother, Amanda. With little compassion, Hiram once again, debated his father's decision to abandon his mother in her hour of need and the after effects of his choice— his father falling victim to the deadly yellow fever during his absence.

Hiram's grandfather, Geoffrey Edward McDonnally, was a veteran as well, serving as an officer in the Crimean War. The gallantry and respect that came with serving were insufficient lures to draw Hiram to the profession. Having observed the impact of the military on the McDonnally clan, Hiram had balked at carrying on the family tradition and remained a civilian. Being a pacifist avoiding what he termed "violent death and destruction," there was a strong possibility that Captain Geoffrey Lachlan McDonnally would be the last of the fallen McDonnally soldiers.

Hiram's search for a pleasant memory ended in the parlor, as he fumbled with a small wooden box, found on the parlor table, whose ghostly covering had appeared to have been tossed aside. He held the unsuspecting trinket up to the light stealing through the glazed window. He squinted at it briefly, cracking the lid to peer in at its contents, as one would open the proverbial Pandora's Box. Overwrought, in finding it barren, he collapsed into the over-stuffed chair next to the table, pressing the object of his disappointment to his chest.

It's gone... the only gift from Grandmother. She entrusted it to me. A chilling shiver passed over him, as he visualized the small wilted figure, pleading on her deathbed.

"Hiram... the box, lose it and your life will become meaningless and your self-destruction will follow," she had whispered with struggling breaths. Since then, the verity in her prediction had weighed heavily upon him.

Sarah Glasgow Selrach, Amanda's mother, characteristically "little but mighty", was undeniably "tough as nails" according to her late husband, Alexander. This truth was apparent; she had lived most of her life as a cold, controlling woman, yet her intentions were remarkably honorable and motivated by love.

Hiram studied the lines of the box, remembering the day that his grandmother had presented it to him. He had returned home to the manor to celebrate his father's promotion when Grandma Selrach had discovered him rifling through her roll-top desk in search of kite string. He was met with her harsh reprimand and frightfully grimaced at her disgusted expression, peering over the tambour.

He quickly rolled the top down, while she continued in an unforgiving tone, denouncing his behavior and lecturing him to tears with the "tenets of privacy" and prophetic omens for the future of the common thief. However, the violated grand-mother eventually softened mercifully, when she observed her proud grandson, frantically wiping the relentless stream appearing on his cheeks. She ended the dissertation abruptly and turned to her bureau, to open the top drawer and withdraw the small wooden box. She then, offered the unusual gift to the sniffling menace and with a forgiving smile lighting her careworn face, she commanded, "Now, be happy, little one; take this; the answer is here and no more regrets young Hiram."

Hiram, humbly, relived the embarrassment and the relief which had followed with his grand-mother's comforting embrace.

He ran his fingers over the fabric of the chair, recalling the candlelight hours that he had spent sitting there, scribbling parchment messages that denoted locations for clandestine meetings with Naomi. This had been a time when he was im-mersed in the pursuit of his dreams with the most wonderful girl in the British Isles. Hiram sighed and sank deeper into the sun-bleached cabbage-floral cushions and closed his eyes. In retrospect, he con-sidered the disquieting irony of the sweet girl's promises of a future together and the years that had careened past, while they lived in separate worlds.

Opening his eyes, gazing upward, scanning the crown molding that encased the lofty ceiling, he felt small, despite his large stature. However, the deafening silence in the parlor was no stranger to him. His past reclusive life had been nearly void of conversation, working alone in the back of the repair shop without contact with the customers. His mundane existence in Switzerland had hinged on his apathy to life in general, living as a mere machine, without hope, motivation, or inspiration. Tonight, aware that his stoicism was uncomfortably fading with the ambiance of his childhood home, he made every effort to curtail any further lapse into self-pity, by leaving the parlor and dreaded foyer, to retire for the evening.

Hiram lit the lamp, found on the bookcase, to assist in the climb upstairs. Guided by the oak railing, he moved up the winding staircase, like a spirit lost in time. He emerged into the second floor hall, passing through a gallery of oils, depicting the McDonnally family line stately displayed on the walls between the many bedrooms. The flickering flame, within the antiquated glass lantern that he held before him, illuminated the solemn faces of his ancestors, all apparently disapproving of the delay in his return. Ignoring their mental lashings, he continued, further disturbed by the fact that these men and women, who had once seemed ancient in his youthful view, now shared his middle age.

Severing himself from his abhorrent past, he hastened his pace, maneuvering through the dark hall, seeking the entry to his bedroom of past years, by the single beacon fluttering playfully, with each step.

A glimpse of the silhouette of a woman, framed by the large opened window in the master bedroom, drew him to the doorway. Assuming that the figure was that of the caretaker's wife, he stepped inside the room to have a closer look, "Mrs. Zigmann?" The woman in question pivoted from the shadows, at his command, with an unexpected response.

"Hello, Hiram," the familiar voice faintly quavered, revealing her identity.

"Naomi?"

Chapter 11

"The Encounter"

"Is it thy will thy image
should keep open
My heavy eyelids
to the weary night?
Dost thou desire my slumbers
Should be broken
While shadows like to thee
Do mock my sight?"

— William Shakespeare

Hiram stood with narrowed eyes, piercing the immobile shadow, desperately trying to rationalize Naomi's presence after decades void of any communication with her. A thundering onslaught of questions pounded in his head, clouding his ability to think clearly, igniting the silent rage smoldering deep within his motionless body. He stood feeling claustrophobic by the guarded anger and betrayal, tightening around his neck.

Naomi took one hesitant step closer, toward the stunned figure and pleaded, "Hiram..."

Moving through the darkness, she reached out to him. He shook his head, trembling, backing over the threshold away from her, with his heart racing. Short of breath, with the pressure of the unexpected encounter, he fled to his bedroom of years gone by. His nemesis shivering in the moonlight, stood catatonic in the chilling, dark hollow of the room for several minutes, paralyzed by the brevity of the meeting.

He was standing in the same room with me...after all these years. She studied the spot where he had stood, disappointed and distressed. The moment, with the only man she had ever loved, was not less than fleeting. Nothing was resolved; nothing had changed. These truths snuffed out the glimmer of hope that had encouraged her to return to McDonnally Manor, a month earlier. Naomi floated, helplessly, in the shadows, a sole survivor on a sea of desperation. Her sense of failure and aloneness was further exasperated by the vastness of the large room with oversized furnishings.

She remained briefly, then found her way over to the wicker basket on the floor, next to the dressing table. There, she lifted a rather large black and gray striped cat from its dreams of kitten days, and cradled it in her arms, then spoke softly, "Oh, Patience... maybe we shouldn't have come."

Naomi found the edge of the ebony four-poster bed, then slowly lowered her head to the down pillow and curled up with her loving companion. The fifteen-year-old cat, a gift from Hiram's uncle, Edward, her late husband, was given to her as a reminder that her dream would come true. In time, she would be reunited with his nephew, Hiram; she just needed to be "patient." However, tonight's episode seemed to give little credence to Edward's past optimism for her future with Hiram.

The appearance of shadows from the oak leaves dancing across the windowpanes, choreographed by the summer breeze, took her back to an October afternoon in the garden of the village churchyard. There, Hiram, a handsome, lanky lad of fourteen had been teasing her incessantly about her poor training in horsemanship.

Yes, my riding abilities were not quite up to snuff, back then, she admitted. While imagining the young Hiram chasing her with fists full of leaves, laughing and mocking her, a gleam formed in her eye; *he kissed me that day, my first kiss.* When she stumbled over the flagstone, he rushed to her side, lifting her to her feet, and then sweetly kissed her scraped forehead.

She stared into the eyes of the purring pet, "His eyes, his amazing dark eyes were filled with regret, he had felt responsible for my injury that day," her words floated through the night. He had made a solid covenant to protect her for the rest of his life. Recapping her quandary, Naomi rolled over, staring at the slightly opened door to the hall. Patience laid coiled on the pillow next to hers, Hiram a room away. Unable to reach him, Naomi began sobbing; knowing the truth that she had harbored for nearly twenty years had to be known.

"Tomorrow," she whispered, then drifted off.

In the adjoining, nautically decorated, bedroom, Hiram lay fully dressed on top of the tartan comforter, deciphering the unexpected events of the last hour. The curtains rippled intermittently, like waves lapping on the shore, failing to break his focus on a bright star, appearing in the upper right pane, which he unconsciously addressed.

What is she doing here? To pour salt over my wounds?! Is she turning to me now, because Edward's gone?! Blast her!

He scanned the night sky, in search of an answer, and then returned to study the celestial gem that shone brighter than the neighboring clusters.

Trying to attain a proper perspective, Hiram mentally rationalized, *Naomi is older. She has to be.* But he never saw her face; that angelic face, engraved in his memory since that first encounter at the market. He recollected that she was not beautiful by society's standards, but retained purity in her smile and radiated warmth with every word that she had spoken. She had a spiritual-like quality superior to all the women he had known, save his grandmother. And over the years, he had yearned for the soft, gentle touch of Naomi's youthful hands, caressing *his* face. He had missed her contagious vigor for life that predominated the innocent nights that they had shared.

Contrite thoughts reared, *I would have never subjected her to those late-night rendezvous, if Uncle*

Edward would have accepted the relationship. Naomi's father had no problem with it. Of course, Edward never gave us his blessing; the blasted devil wanted Naomi for himself!

Hiram had lived with the deplorable belief that his uncle had fabricated the claims of her gold digging nature, to mask his own amorous feelings for her. He suffered from two ultimate betrayals: having been denied the sanctuary of his home and Naomi having become his uncle's wife. Now, his emotions were mixed and the future indeterminate, upon recovering the former and addressing the latter. Hiram had loved Naomi more than life itself, but now he resented her very presence in the mansion. He turned toward the large double windows that loomed over the estate.

He had thought that she was perfect in every sense of the word, a demigoddess incapable of such horrid deception. He pondered this question with impunity, time and time again. *How could she? All of the blatant lies!* The unbearable, logical deduction that Naomi had chosen his mature, handsome uncle, endowed with wealth and security, continued to haunt him.

I was too young, I had nothing to offer her, I had no choice, but to leave her! The undeniable reality was that his Banishment had come four years short of his receiving the scheduled inheritance and he never returned to claim it. His eyes closed with visions of his strong, youthful hand tearing the calendar from the wall on his twenty-first birthday, cursing the very day that he was born, the promised fortune and McDonnally Manor. His birthright had become of little interest to him, yet remained to be a searing thorn in his side of obliterated dreams.

At this point, there was only one thing that Hiram was certain of; if Naomi had not been a McDonnally by marriage, Edward's widow, he would have had her removed from the manor with immediacy and without reservation. The debilitating stress of the culmination of his unsettling past prevailed, as he nodded off.

Chapter 111

"The Truth"

"A perfect Woman, nobly planned
To warn, to comfort,
And command;
And yet a Spirit still, and bright
With something of angelic light."

— William Wordsworth

In the heat of the morning sun, Patience was
earnestly watching the birds in the garden, from
the window seat, when the adjacent bedroom door
slammed, waking Naomi from a night of already
broken slumber. It was utterly apparent to the unwelcome house guest that Hiram's mood had not
improved, nor was he compelled to exonerate her.
Refusing to accept defeat, Naomi, hurried to the
dressing table and sat down on the eyelet lace covered bench, to prepare for a second chance to make
amends. She shifted to reposition herself in front of
the mirror, met by the scarred face that reflected
back at her, exhibiting the elongated mark that ran
from the corner of her left temple down to her chin.

She ran her index finger down the scarred
path and questioned, *Will he ever love me again?*
She consulted the woman in the mirror, who
shared a remarkable resemblance to her mother;
with even the tiny inherited dimple in her right
cheek. She shook her head, resolved to the fact that
any future with Hiram would be God's decision. She
sat back, staring at the young-looking woman of
thirty-four, and proceeded to brush her thick,
shoulder-length hair and pinned up her auburn
locks with a silver barrette. After which, she took a
moment of silent prayer for guidance in handling
the arduous task ahead and asked for forgiveness
for her negligence in attending to the deception
sooner.

With a smile and a renewed perspective,
Naomi chose a bright blue frock and the crocheted
shawl, which she had purchased at a small back-
street shop in London, bathed and dressed. She
carried Patience down the maid's stairs to the aus-

tere, yet sufficiently equipped kitchen for breakfast, half expecting a second encounter with the master. The relentless crowing of the rooster, near the caretaker's cottage in the distance, amused Naomi while she offered the other member of the duet, her mewing friend, a bit of cod and cream. A couple of Eloise's freshly baked lemon tarts lured Naomi to the pantry to treat herself to the steaming pastry. She poured a cup of hot tea from the Wedgwood teapot near the woodstove, and then nervously began breakfast with anticipation of Hiram's appearance.

With his delayed arrival, Naomi prolonged her meal with Patience, until a half hour had passed, then set out to search the somewhat dismal interior of the mansion, with hope of locating her troubled soul mate. Upon reaching the third floor, she wandered into the mesmerizing ballroom, an elegant, spacious room adorned with three, Italian, crystal chandeliers. Their prismatic light, waltzed cheerfully on the pale blue, plaster walls, with each renewed breeze that swept through the enormous veranda doors, which the caretaker's wife, Eloise, opened daily in order to air the cavernous chamber.

Naomi was admiring the detail of the tin ceiling, when the tapping of a hammer, drew her to the room below where she found Mr. Zigmann, Eloise's husband. The caretaker and his wife were employed to live in the manor's cottage, shortly after Edward and Naomi were married. The white-haired, sixty-year-old, stood tall in the small bedroom repairing a cornice. Burly, Albert Zigmann stepped down from the ladder, motioning with the hammer; while he offered an explanation that he had driven Hiram to the rail station to take the train to the northern borough of Lankford.

Naomi excused herself, returned to the kitchen, and chose another lemon tart to console herself after the news of the postponed meeting with Hiram. Preoccupied, she finished the pastry, without knowledge of its delightful flavor and decided, half-heartedly, to take the opportunity to stroll through the once lush gardens behind the mansion. While she followed the maze of stone paths, she imagined the beauty that the grounds bestowed in another life; a garden adorned with aromatic roses, snapdragons and Marybuds. With her hands on her hips, she examined the result of years of neglect.

Allison could work miracles with this place, with her green thumb, she pondered, considering a resurrection of the flora disaster. Naomi recalled that Allison had a great love of the outdoors. This had been apparent since that precious day in London, after the adoption proceedings when they spent the entire day celebrating in St. James Park.

Naomi's thoughts reverted to Hiram; she was certain that he would love Allison as much as she did.

How could anyone, not love Allison? She is life in all its splendor and grace, she thought proudly.

Her adopted daughter had grown into a blonde, blue-eyed, gregarious beauty of twenty-three with an intoxicating joy for life and an infectious smile. Allison was a gift from Heaven, delivered to Naomi in her most desperate hours, to change both their lives. From that first special moment, Allison mended Naomi's broken heart and squelched her new mother's self-pity with an un-conditional love; the precocious little girl reached up, patted her mother's damaged face, whispering softly, "I love you, my mummy." That loving ges-ture marked the dawn of Naomi's new life, in which she would no longer be self-absorbed with her aber-rant appearance. Within months, she had regained the confidence to work publicly, assisting with the tutoring of the disabled at the village orphanage. In the years to follow, she broadened the opportunities of many of Allison's unfortunate peers, destined by their cruel fate to become little more than illiterate beggars.

Naomi had made a nurturing home for Alli-son with the help of her late husband, Edward, who provided mother and daughter with a charming white-washed cottage on the outskirts of London. After Edward and Naomi exchanged vows, he re-mained in Paris, with infrequent, late evening visits to London, primarily to avoid contact with Allison. Edward was altruistic with his time and monthly allotments, but had chosen to remain anonymous to Naomi's daughter; a tragedy in Naomi's opinion, believing that he too, would have benefited from the love of the blessed foundling.

As Allison grew, the allotments increased and Edward's visits decreased. He provided everything possible for Naomi and Allison, but took nothing in return; he felt that he deserved nothing. Likewise, he had insisted that Allison keep her surname, O'Connor, sincerely claiming that she needed to maintain her family roots, not his. Naomi initially took offense to this demand, but realized that she was in no position to argue the point.

The seven years that had passed since Naomi had seen or had spoken with Edward, were finalized by his last request after he succumbed to pneumonia; no one was to be present at his private burial. This was another request that Naomi had felt obliged to honor which had personally offended her.

Naomi now clinging to the wrought iron gate, which led to the courtyard, witnessed a pair of bluebirds, flitting playfully above the uninhabited aviary. *A pleasant omen for us?* she queried, *Maybe there is hope for Hiram and me.* She eyed the sparkling dew on the arborvitaes that bordered the brick paths, leading to the meadow where the neighbor's horses grazed.

Master of Brachney Hall, he's a mysterious man. He was seldom seen at his home or anywhere else, for that matter. *He too wore a beard*, she remembered, except that even from a distance, his was a striking, sunset red. She had never made his acquaintance. The rest of the community, found him to be elusive and evasive.

Naomi sat down on the cool stone bench, eroded by a century of spring rains, avoiding the green moss at one end. She shielded her eyes, with her hand as she peered out across the meadow, enjoying the warmth of the summer sun and remembering that dreadful day when the mercury had reached the one-hundred degree mark in London, two years earlier.

She looked toward the cloudless sky, consulting with her beloved Maker, seeking the correct words, to convey the story behind her marriage to Hiram's uncle. Naomi prayed for another opportunity to convince Hiram that her marriage, an irreversible part of the past, had been a necessary one in the course of events. This reasoning stemmed from the council that she had received in a letter from Hiram's pious grandmother, Sarah. Naomi mentally recited the invaluable phrase, authored by the wise woman.

"You will be inoculated from further despair, if you accept the termination of a once treasured relationship and realize the necessity of that experience to the development of successful, future relationships." Naomi was humbled, knowing that she too, should concede to this advice, if Hiram responded negatively, once again.

A genteel woman's voice interrupted her thoughts, "If you please Mum, the Master would like to see you in the parlor."

A trifle astonished by the request, an immediate answer to her prayer, Naomi thanked Eloise and mentally prepared herself for the second "meeting" with Hiram.

How could this be? He does care. He's returned from Lankford. She stood up, smoothed the wrinkles from her skirt, took a deep breath and walked with a steady gait and a conscientious attitude toward the main house.

I owe Edward my life, so does Hiram; he needs to know the truth

Naomi found the parlor pleasantly prepared for guests, no longer hidden beneath cobwebs or furniture covers. Hiram was pacing nervously, checking his pocket watch when she arrived. She entered the room unnoticed and seated herself in the over-stuffed chair, then began unconsciously assessing the mature characteristics of the man, the former, vibrant youth whom she had loved. She analyzed his physical attributes with increased anticipation to see his face, screened in the darkness the night before. Hiram, reviewing the previous meeting with Naomi, paused at the large open windows, overlooking the grounds where the green copper fountain was dry and lifeless.

"You wanted to see, me Hiram?" she broke the silence. Startled, caught off guard, he remained facing the window, fidgeting with his watch.

"Thank you for responding, so quickly," he murmured with cool civility. With an air of apathy, he turned toward his guest. His eyes fixed on the tiny pocket of his vest; he slid the fob through his fingers, mechanically replacing the timepiece. Naomi concerned with the seemingly dark and ominous manner in which he moved and the tone with which he spoke, shifted uncomfortably.

"I have been ..." his words were slow to leave his mouth, as he raised his head, to confront the "face" of his betrayer for the first time. Hiram's mouth dropped and his eyes widened, taken aback by the unsightly scar that modified the once cherished countenance.

Naomi froze, observing his distressed reaction. Having been accustomed to the initial shock of curious onlookers, she normally prepared a defensive, yet charitable response; however, this time it was explicably different. This was the love of her life, this was the one person, who knew her and loved her "before." Her first instinct was to take leave and run as far away as possible, but she too, was absorbed in the new face of the once young lad for whom she had prayed everyday.

They studied each other in suffocating silence, searching for the familiar, when the intensity returned to Hiram's dark eyes, and he blurted, "Did my uncle do this to you?!"

"Oh no, Hiram, it was not like that!" Naomi panicked. With her blatant response, Hiram naturally assumed that her facial injury was the result of an accidental mishap, unaware that, on the contrary, his uncle was very much involved in the incident. Naomi summoned her inner strength and focused on her mission, cautiously offering Hiram the rocking chair, which she pulled next to her.

"Hiram, please sit down," she invited. Hiram reluctantly acquiesced, uncomfortably taking his place beside her, subconsciously aware that a refusal may be offensive. Hiram clenched the arms of the rocker, stabilizing his restless emotions, having difficulty harboring anger towards the Naomi who had dealt with such personal trauma.

He is a very large man now, tall and broad shouldered. His hair has not changed. No signs of gray, just the same head of beautiful black curls, the envy of every girl on the island. Naturally, he matured... but quite gracefully, Naomi mentally noted. She ended the suppressing silence and began confidently with her first thoughts.

"You are still quite handsome, Hiram," she affirmed softly with a placid smile. Hiram tightened his grip, in surprise with the comment, having never believed to be any more than average. His modesty and her altered appearance left him embarrassed, without the option of reciprocating the compliment. He hastily sought an alternative comment, however none came to mind. Observing his plight, with hopes of alleviating his obvious discomfort, Naomi gently reached out to his somber face and touched his cheek as she had done so many times before.

"It's okay Hiram, I'm fine," she assured him tenderly.

The courage in her words was overwhelming. He felt the pressure of his past life without her, building up, deep inside, when the soft, reminiscent caress, unexpectedly, released eighteen years of latent tension, forcing one small tear from his downcast eyes, trickling to her fingers. Hiram fearfully, withdrew from her hand; the pains of the past decades stinging like a recent wound. Her loving touch strapped him to the chair, while his broken heart struggled to be set free. Naomi with natural, motherly intentions, pulled a silk hanky from her sleeve, a white flag of surrender, and blotted his cheek, as well as her own.

Neither party could process what was happening. The mere fact that they were in the same room together was nearly impossible to comprehend; an enigma of confusion, anger, and compassion. The introductory prelude in the master bedroom did little to lessen the enormity of the current situation.

I will not let her do this to me! She will never hurt me again! His conscious quaked. He left the rocker abruptly and returned to the window, shaken by his moment of weakness. Naomi intuitively followed him. Tucking her skirt beneath her, she joined him on the window seat, seeking to diffuse his undeniable resentment. There they sat within arms length. Without further delay, Naomi seized the opportunity to begin unraveling the mystery of the accident and her unlikely marriage to his uncle. Convinced that Divine intervention had reunited them, she spoke with encouraged enthusiasm, confident that Hiram would, most assuredly, understand.

"To begin with, Hiram, my father, Nathan, you probably remember as a very agreeable man... He was in fact, ruthless and calculating." Naomi paused, observing Hiram's curious interest. He envisioned Nathan MacKenzie, the intimidating, large, gray haired, scruffy man who openly welcomed him at every visit to Grimwald.

"Actually, Hiram, in reality, he was consumed with the desire to regain possession of this estate."

Naomi continued with ease, further divulging that her father had believed, emphatically, that he had been cheated, when this acreage, bordering his property at Grimwald, had been awarded to Hiram's family, on completion of the new survey. She explained that Nathan was certain that the old topographic maps presented were, not only inaccurately interpreted, but also accused the magistrate, Hiram's grandfather, of being biased in making the transaction, those years ago. Hiram cocked his head slightly in surprise, unaware of her father's severe disgruntlement.

" I recall, that my grandfather did speak frequently of a property dispute when I was quite young. I wasn't aware that it was with *your* father," Hiram intervened, somewhat surprised, now regaining eye contact.

Maybe we can have a civil conversation; Naomi thought as she continued.

"Yes, it was with my father, Hiram. I can't emphasize enough, how vengeful and obsessive he had become. Not long after Edward had realized that you and I were spending time together, he overheard, Nathan's rogues, regulars at the Tin Cup Tavern, discussing my father's contrived plan for us...after we... after you and I were married." Naomi leaned toward Hiram, now apparently distracted. His thoughts were momentarily disturbed with the word "married."

Married... that was my dream. Hiram remembered.

"Hiram? He was.. he was planning to kill you after our marriage and have me relinquish the estate to him," Naomi spoke matter-of-factly, fingers clenched, anticipating a myriad of possible reactions.

"What?!" Hiram awoke abruptly from the daydream.

"Yes, that was the plan. My father was willing to stoop to the lowest possible means to own McDonnally Manor," Naomi reported with embarrassment, for the family connection.

With this reported threat, Hiram instantly left the window seat, and then paused with knitted brows, scrutinizing the memories and retreated to the corner of the room.

"That's why the blasted fiend found our relationship so appealing!" The dawning of this additional incident of betrayal sent Hiram, with flaring nostrils, and long strides toward the fireplace.

Naomi sat tight, and proceeded, hoping the worst was over. "Yes, Hiram, Edward, too, was infuriated with Nathan's plan. Initially, Edward truly believed that I had played a key role in the conspiracy. That's why he made every effort to end our relationship, yours and mine, to protect you. We were very young then and you were his responsibility;

Edward knew that you would take matters into your own hands and that you were no match for my father... Yes, Edward made you leave your home, and he was afraid that you headed to Grimwald. He never anticipated that you would just disappear."

Naomi continued, explaining that after Hiram left the manor that, Edward set out to find him and confront her and her father at Grimwald, outraged that the conniving pair had forced his hand in banishing his own flesh and blood.

"It was not until he had interrogated Nathan at our home that morning, that Edward discovered my innocence in the scheme."

Naomi continued the saga, pointing out how Edward's pacifism was lost to agitation, when Nathan, in a drunken stupor, had laughed and had spat on him. After which, her father had pulled his knife from his belt, threatening to end Edward's life.

"My brother Jeremiah was huddling in the corner, crying," Naomi added sadly.

"That insidious, vile savage!" Hiram interjected, slamming his fist down on the mantle.

"Hiram!" Naomi unconsciously reprimanded.

Hiram turned away from her, rubbing his fist and began pacing, simmering with the anger that he knew was gradually gaining control.

Noting his escalated vexation, Naomi continued, albeit reluctantly, to explain that, Edward, had fearfully lunged for the fireplace poker in his defense. Naomi rose from the window seat as she spoke and fell into a trance-like state, reliving that fateful moment when the hook of the poker had caught the side of her face when Edward swung it upward, at the very moment that she stepped in to intervene.

"Hiram, it was horrible. It just kept coming. Everything was red. My hands, I couldn't see my hands... My skirt, the carpet, his shirt; it was everywhere. The pain, I couldn't stand the pain. And the noise; everyone was yelling. Everything was dark red..."

Naomi found herself standing silently in the parlor, staring blankly at her open hands. Hiram stood motionless, shocked by the unexpected display. He stepped over to awaken her from the nightmare at Grimwald, placing his hands on her shoulders, fighting the urge to embrace her with a comforting hug. Instead his large hands pressed her gently down to the seat, and then moved to his forehead where they appeared to be massaging the confusion from his brain, sliding back over his dark curls to rest on the back of his neck. He stared upward in disbelief, shaking his head with disapproval for Naomi's foolish attempt in diplomacy.

Naomi, snapped back to reality, embarrassed by her dramatic account and apologized. She returned to her explanation of the incident, now recounting that within minutes of the blow, she had fallen into shock, which resulted in her passing out.

Edward had later explained to her that directly after the accident, Nathan had gone into a full-fledged series of cursing threats and claims to the McDonnally estate for restitution, with no concern for his daughter's well-being. Without further delay, Edward had hit Nathan's wrist and then, in that desperate moment, when the knife hit the floor and Nathan went for it, he had laid a firm punch to her father's face.

"Edward, then, scooped me up and rushed me to the attending doctor in the next village."

Naomi pleaded with an expression of sincere gratitude, "Hiram, all of Edward's plans to reconcile with
you vanished with my accident. Your uncle was a
good man; he sacrificed his life and his happiness,
to care for me, believing the responsibility was
justly his."

Naomi glanced upward, "He had insisted that
we marry to protect my reputation. It was obvious
that I could no longer live with Jeremiah and my
father and I felt that any future for marital bliss
had been ripped from me with the stroke of that
poker... Oh yes, there was a wedding... I remember
fragments of it: the stranger holding my hand, the
obscuring veil and the promises." Naomi searched
Hiram's eyes for a glimmer of understanding from
her lost love.

"Not that I'm ungrateful Hiram, but Edward
and I never lived as man and wife. He respected me.
He never would have taken advantage of the situation. He arranged for me to stay in a cottage near
London, while he lived in Paris, when he wasn't
traveling with business."

Hiram looked away briefly, confused and
withdrawn, running his hand across his beard. He
flashed back through the years, realizing that his
malevolent feelings for his late uncle were partially
unfounded, which painfully expedited the forthcom-
ing explosion. The intensity increased with the disturbing implication that his life was merely a point-
less response to what he considered an illegitimate
case for matrimony.

He moved away from Naomi, who now sat
wringing her hands in anguish, believing that their
fate was now in *his* hands. Her eyes nervously
trailed his movements as he began traversing the

room aimlessly, indirectly destined back toward the fireplace.

With a cautious, yet melancholy tone, Naomi sullenly concluded, "I know that you probably read in the society columns that Edward and I were married, but they failed to report that Edward and I were not living as husband and wife. Hiram, we were never in love," she desperately reiterated. "We shared a mutual respect for one another," she added, making one last effort to support her case.

Hiram stood with one hand on the aged fireplace mantel, staring into the dark cavern behind the hearth; his breathing becoming deep and deliberate. Naomi moved slowly from the window seat to console him, silently crossing the room, with the precaution of one treading on shards of glass. In an unexpected instant, Hiram whipped around toward her and in an earthshaking bellow, retaliated.

"What about respect for *me*?! Respect for my trust, respect for *my* life?!" He subconsciously seized the poker, and began punishing the responsible tool, violently rapping the hearth tiles with each tormented word.

"I have spent the last *eighteen* years as a God forsaken *hermit*, mourning a love and a life that I lost with *you*! You did not even have the courtesy to inform me that your selfish marriage was a marriage of convenience! You never gave me the opportunity to console you! You left me to believe that our love was a one-sided sham and that I was a fool! Well, I was, wasn't I?!"

Hiram continued beating the tiles, mercilessly, shattering the pieces that sprayed through the air and rained down around him and his horrified, lost love.

"I thought that I knew you! I trusted you with my life and you destroyed it!" he roared. He raised his head, wielding the tool one last time to the floor.

"Why, Naomi? Why?!" his face flooded with tears, his vision blurred. "I would have taken care of you! I loved you Nomee! I loved you!"

Naomi's heart screamed, "*Help him!*" but her fear deterred her; shrieking back at the sight of the threatening poker. Seeing the terror in her face with the tool ironically grasped in his hand, Hiram cast it forcefully towards the grate, to be swallowed by the darkness.

He ran his sleeve across his face, heaved over the small table and stormed out of the parlor, followed by Naomi's cry. "No Hiram! No!" she begged him to return.

Hiram left the mansion and Naomi once again.

"I loved you too, Hiram," she called to the closed door. Naomi stood trembling, "Please God, not again." She fell to sobbing uncontrollably for several minutes, shaken and drained. She up-righted the table and lowered herself into the rocker, staring at the shattered tile, strewn around the room, now filled with silence. She began to rock gently, defeated and disillusioned, imagining how devastated Hiram was feeling at that very moment.

Dear God, what have I done? Now he regrets more than losing me, he regrets his entire life. With that brutal reality, she dropped her head to her hands, while the stream of tears fell passed over the scar to her lap. She raised her head, removed her handkerchief from her sleeve, and examined it briefly. She gently caressed the cloth, dampened with Hiram's tears, and pressed it against her cheek.

God forsaken hermit? She never dreamed that he had pined for her all those years. Naomi surveyed the room, revisiting each spot that Hiram shared during the confrontation, when her eyes fell on the small wooden box, laying next to the sofa. She left the safety of the chair to retrieve the treasure and return it to its rightful place on the table beside her. She ran her fingers across the smooth edges of the chest, desperately praying for an answer.

The box, Sarah's legacy, was a haunting reminder that she may have committed a grave disservice to her memory. Naomi would often venture from Grimwald to meet with Hiram and then while waiting for his arrival she would chat with his grandmother Sarah in the village teashop. Sarah emphasized the necessity of spiritual advancement and aiding those in need. Those conversations proved to be quite beneficial later, promoting the confidence and forgiveness that Naomi lacked after the accident.

Naomi pondered; *quite possibly, it is my responsibility to ameliorate the lifestyle of Sarah's grandson. My actions sent him on this faithless path. I cannot give up... I will try again... I have to.*

Naomi scanned the room and walked with dread and a heavy heart toward the pantry to retrieve the necessary utensils to dispose of the aftermath in the parlor. Eloise met her in the hall, where she gently lifted the broom and dustbin from Naomi's trembling hands.

"Oh, Mum," is all the loving maid could say, before Naomi wept openly in the arms of the sympathetic older woman. "Don't lose faith, Mum... go on upstairs and get some rest, I'll tend to the cleanup," Eloise benevolently suggested, unaware of the magnitude of the work ahead of her.

Naomi reluctantly agreed, thanked Eloise, and then longingly started up the staircase to return to the bedroom. There she found her cat perched once again on the sill, fascinated by activity in the garden below. Armed with renewed hope and believing Hiram to be the source of the cat's entertainment, Naomi hurried to join Patience at the window. Instead she discovered that the strange red-bearded neighbor was staring up at her from the meadow, holding the lead rope of his large bay Percheron.

Naomi, not quite sure how to respond, whether to wave or pretend that she had not noticed him, turned shyly away momentarily. She then returned a glance back to the meadow, surprised to find that the neighbor was fixed in his position, smiling up at her. Doubts surfaced, then she considered that he may have been actually examining the edifice. Still feeling self-conscious after her encounter with Hiram, she cautiously brought her hand to her cheek to conceal the scar, still moist with tear drops; ashamed of her vanity, she immediately lowered her hand. Then it happened; he waved. She felt that proper etiquette demanded that she return the greeting, so she gestured, gently.

After the exchange, the mysterious man led his horse away, while Naomi watched, perplexed, and temporarily removed from her former troubles with Hiram. She returned to cuddle with Patience on the settee. "Oh, Patience, in ten minutes, I have one bearded man, angrily bidding me farewell and another, happily greeting me... life is so confusing." They sat for several minutes before Naomi's priorities sent her thoughts back to Hiram and the purpose for her stay at McDonnally Manor.

A sudden cold draft from the window brought her attention to the dark eastern sky, which was blackening with alarming rapidity. With the storm brewing, she rushed to the window for one final search for Hiram and to scan the meadow for the horses. She was frustrated to see no sign of the manor's master, but was pleased to find that the Master of Brachney Hall, mysterious owner of the four handsome equines, had safely returned them to the barn.

Now, the deep ebony swirling sky filtered the daylight from the manor. Naomi fought to close the windows as the rushing sound of the threatening winds filled the room. She quickly lit the kerosene lamp on the dressing table and carried it to the darkened hall, suspecting that Hiram was probably somewhere on the grounds, ranting and raving over their meeting. She hurried over to descend the stairs, when the door from the adjacent bedroom slammed, from an unexpected gust. The loud crack sent Patience in a simultaneous dash for the top step; within a split second, they became entangled, knocking Naomi off balance. The young woman tumbled down the stairs, with the kerosene from the lantern, splashing into her face and her equally surprised pet, rolling close behind. With a blood-curdling scream, Naomi and Patience met the parquet floor below.

Chapter IV

"The Voice"

"The boat has left
a stormy land.
A stormy sea before her,
When, O! too strong for
human hand,
The tempest gather'd
o'er her."

— Thomas Campbell

Days went by at McDonnally Manor, while solemn eyes watched over the convalescent, now confined to the large featherbed in the master bedroom. Thankfully, she was slowly regaining consciousness, after a long harrowing week of intensive care with her scrapes cleaned and her eyes rinsed. Although the restrictive bandages, now wrapped around her head, prevented the frustrated patient from opening her eyes, Naomi's worst fears were dismissed when a familiar, male voice reassured her that her sight was in good order. It also warned that the physician had left orders for her eyes to remain covered until the end of the week.

Later, Eloise explained to the semi-conscious woman, that the man with the Voice was attending her by day and she by night. Naomi vaguely remembered the accident and was very confused by the man's Voice, trying desperately, but unsuccessfully, to put a face with it. She attempted to speak coherently, but only managed to deliver a one-word question, with her foremost concern, "Patience?"

Eloise placed Naomi's hand on the ball of fur curled up on her right. "Not to worry, she's doing just fine." Naomi managed a faint smile and promptly fell back to sleep with her loving pet.

The next morning, Naomi awoke startled once again by the head wraps. The familiar Voice reiterated that the bandages were temporary and bid her a good morning, then inquired as to how she was feeling.

Naomi instantly replied with a smile, "I'm famished!"

"Wonderful, I'll fetch your breakfast," the Voice, announced fading from the room.

"Wait, sir!" Naomi called out; but there was no response. For a moment, she thought that she was dreaming, but Patience's purring beneath her hand affirmed that she was not.

"Oh, Payshe, I'm so glad that you weren't injured," she declared, when suddenly, she felt a tiny bandage on her friend's left paw. "Oh, my poor baby, not you too?" a second of panic ran through her. Naomi snuggled close to the mewing empathetic victim to wait for the Voice to return with her meal, while thoughts, of her daughter Allison, the accident, the horses, and the neighbor kept her busy. The Voice arrived with a bowl of steaming porridge, an oatcake, bangers (sausages) topped with quince jelly, and a cup of tea.

"It smells delightful!" Naomi sat up straight, preparing her taste buds for the first delectable meal, since her fall.

"If you please, here's your first bite of porridge," the Voice offered the patient, who had been subsisting on an occasional ration of chicken broth. Naomi eagerly took the spoonful, followed by a sip of tea.

"This is a very difficult, uncommon situation...anticipating the next bite, that is," Naomi commented between mouthfuls, justifying her awkwardness.

"I'll cue you in advance. Just open your mouth when you feel the spoon touch your lips," the Voice suggested, while blotting the corners of Naomi's mouth with the napkin.

"Thank you. It's quite a challenge; trying to be a vision of grace, when you're being fed like a helpless fledgling." Naomi made a discreet search for the napkin, feeling a drip of jelly escaping down her chin, when her hand fell on that of her attendant. Naomi sat silently as her fingers curiously explored the back of the large, strong hand, when the Voice inquired, "May, I help you find something?"

Naomi immediately withdrew her hand, too embarrassed to reply. The hand in question efficiently wiped the trace of condiment from her face.

"I'm sorry." Naomi could feel, the heat rising beneath the bandages. Her slight headache, a symptom of the mild concussion from the fall, became increasingly worse with the embarrassment.

"More hot tea?" the Voice encouraged. Naomi nodded when he placed the cup in her hands. While she savored the tea, the attendant served a small bowl of yesterday's lobster to the impatient, but grateful, feline accomplice in the accident. Naomi devoured one banger and the oatcake before her stomach refused another crumb. She sipped the remainder from the cup, when the mysterious man announced, "Excuse me, I'll be returning the tray to the kitchen now."

"Wait sir! I know that we have met before and I realize that you are enjoying this game of hide and seek, but I've been solving mysteries since I was a young girl. If you please, stay a moment longer. You need not reveal your identity; I'm certain that I can solve this mystery." Naomi confidently reported.

"Reveal it to you? I don't remember saying that I would." The Voice's tone suggested his obvious amusement with her presumption.

"Very well, kind sir, as I pointed out, I need but a few more minutes with you and then I am certain, that I can successfully remove your disguise; strange thing for me to be saying, since I'm donning the mask," Naomi smiled.

"Now, if you please, just repeat these phrases: Shall I post this note for you today? Please humor me. It will only take a moment."

The Voice obliged, pleased to see the woman in such good spirits. Naomi resolved that it belonged to neither the village clerk, nor Mr. Wiggins, the butcher, and concurred that their presence at her bedside, was notably a bit far fetched.

"No, no... I can't think clearly. You have an English accent. But I too have one and I am a Scot. I was raised at Landseer Crag... Wait, one more try?" she implored. "Repeat: Would you prefer the ivory damask or the white linen?" The Voice echoed her words. Naomi listened intently, and then decided to rule out the dry goods merchant imported from London.

"Good day, my lady." The Voice faded into the hall.

Frustrated, Naomi ended the futile investigation, surrendering to a now, splitting headache and loss of her subject. She could pursue the matter no further, leaned back, exhausted, to the comfort of the down pillow. She lamented that she had fallen to the whims of the mystery feeling that her time would have been better spent expressing her gratitude for the accommodating service.

Eloise passed her assistant in the hall and bid him "good morning" then entered the bedroom a few minutes later to change Naomi's bedclothes. Finding her patient resting peacefully with her faithful pet, she tucked the comforter around the sleeping beauties and then tiptoed out to get some much-needed rest, in the adjoining bedroom.

Later that afternoon, a spat between Eloise and "That Cat" (as Eloise referred to it) awakened Naomi. Near full recovery, Patience resumed her favored position atop the large curtain rod, mischievously laying in wait for the bustling Mrs. Zigmann.

"Is Patience misbehaving, Eloise?" Naomi chuckled, feeling well-rested and no longer suffering from the excruciating head pains.

Eloise laughed, "I wish she'd find a field mouse or something to play with, and stop tormenting me with her surprise attacks. I'll bet you're hungry young lady, it's nearly tea time."

"I'm fine, Eloise. I had plenty for breakfast and I don't get too much in the way of exercise, you know." Naomi ran the satin binding through her fingers, then mustered up enough courage to ask the one question, of which she dreaded the answer, "Eloise, where's Hiram?"

"Mum, he's been gone, since noon of the day of your accident. He left with no knowledge of your fall."

"To where, Eloise?"

"I don't know Mum, he left no word."

Naomi sat upright, "Sir are *you* here?" probing the darkness for the Voice.

"No, Mum, he left after he served your breakfast," Eloise verified.

"Will he be returning?" she inquired with a trace of disappointment.

"I don't believe so, Mum. Your bandages will soon be removed and we will no longer need his assistance."

"But Eloise, I didn't get to thank him properly."

"Don't you worry, he's a very understanding and generous man," Eloise reassured her, as Naomi dropped carefully back against the headboard.

"Eloise, who is he?" she implored cautiously.

"Why he's the neighbor, Mum," she revealed, standing beside the bed with one hand gripping the bedpost looming near Naomi's head.

Naomi leaned closer to her informant, "Neighbor? Which neighbor? It wasn't Joseph Dugan."

"My dear, the Master of Brachney Hall," Eloise announced.

Naomi clutched the comforter in surprise, "The gentleman with the red beard?"

Eloise confirmed his identity and continued with her duties, folding the top quilt, which she placed at the foot of the bed.

"How extraordinary, why would he take time to care for me?" Naomi queried suspiciously, wondering if his generosity may have been fueled by her previous acknowledgement at the window.

"Why not, Mum? I guess he felt that it was his neighborly duty; he is an awfully nice chap. He knew that Mr. Zigmann had his hands full with the painting and that I would find it a difficult task to look after you, twenty- four hours a day."

"Oh, Eloise, I have not even thanked you," she reached into space, seeking the arms of the maid. The women exchanged hugs. Naomi, still suffering from some degree of memory loss, asked if the mistress of Brachney Hall had visited during her period of unconsciousness. Eloise paused and reminded her that Lucas McClurry was a bachelor and shared his home with only his groundskeeper.

Eloise went to the pantry to retrieve tea and baps (Scottish bread) spread with blackberry and apple jam, to satiate Naomi's appetite until supper. Having never made prior acquaintance to the Master of Brachney Hall, Naomi mulled over the predicament of the benevolent neighbor's puzzling voice.

Maybe I've confused him with someone else? Or I overheard him speaking with someone in town? It's probably just my head knocked out of kilter by the fall, Naomi deduced. Either way, it was a frustrating situation for the woman who had spent many hours reading mysteries and had successfully solved them before the last chapter.

Eloise served the refreshments and then carefully helped her patient into a fresh gown; Naomi suffered from a number of bruises and moved with difficulty as Eloise dressed her.

"I feel like an infant, being fed and dressed," Naomi sighed. "I'm so bored with the darkness, I can't wait until tomorrow. When is the doctor coming to remove this blindfold, Eloise?" she asked anxiously.

"Have patience, Mum." At that moment, the cat turned and mewed, peering at the maid. Eloise shook her head at the incorrigible cat while Naomi giggled at the feline's response to its name.

"The doctor is scheduled to arrive sometime, late tomorrow afternoon, Mum. Maryanne Wheaton gave birth to a tiny daughter yesterday; a little bit of a thing, born nearly nine weeks early. He'll need to examine them first."

"Nine weeks? That's quite early. Is Patience sunbathing on the windowsill?" Eloise verified that the cat was now comfortably outstretched on the cool granite, observing the activity in the garden below.

"She's watching Mr. Zigmann, conversing with the neighbor."

Naomi sat back, trying to hide her interest, and interjected innocently, "What do you expect they are discussing, Eloise?"

With curious hesitation, Eloise stepped closer to the window and slowly discerned, "It appears that the neighbor dons a beautiful, new lace bonnet and Mr. Zigmann is somewhat undecided as to whether or not he approves of it."

"What?" Naomi moved quickly to the edge of the bed, in spite of her injuries. "Are you sure, Eloise?"

"Oh yes, Mum, that is definitely a new bonnet. I am sure of it; it has pansies on it," she replied nonchalantly, placing the soiled laundry that she had gathered into the muslin-lined basket.

"Do you mean to say that you've seen him wearing lace bonnets before?" Naomi's neck craned toward the window.

Eloise hesitated, reviewed the strange question, laundry basket in hand, and stared silently, perplexed with raised eyebrows at the masked woman. Eloise then broke into uncontrolled laughter until the tears rolled. Dropping the basket, she continued bent over, wiping her eyes with her apron, while Naomi sat in a state of total confusion. Eloise managed to squeeze out a few words in between breaths, "Naomi, it's, it's Harriet Dugan!" Naomi blushed beneath the bandages and joined in the laughter, a bit embarrassed by her preoccupation with the *neighbor*.

Eloise exited the room with her laundry basket, leaving Naomi to plan for the anticipated upcoming days, when she would be released from her bondage. Her priorities with Hiram had comfortably eased their way to the "back burner" with the increasing interest in the mysterious Lucas McClurry.

Naomi gained new respect for the blind, having had spent much of her free time, reading and sketching, prior to the accident. Friday arrived, not a moment to soon for the patient; another day of confinement would have been unbearable. Naomi felt ingratiated to Eloise and her cat, the only sources of amusement, since the neighbor had returned to Brachney Hall. She longed to walk through the garden, impoverished as it was, and even imagined borrowing the bay from the neighbor to go for a peaceful ride, across the moors.

She slid down beneath the comforter, in hopes of falling asleep to lessen the hours, until the bandages would be removed and within a quarter hour, Naomi was enveloped in visions of cantering across the meadow with Hiram and Allison by her side and the red-bearded neighbor, waving in the distance. Her fantasy was abruptly interrupted, with a hand, gently squeezing hers.

"Sorry, Mum, are you sleeping?" This was a common inquiry of late, with Naomi's eyes hidden below the gauze.

"Mum, would you like to hear the letter, which you just received from your lovely daughter?" Eloise asked eagerly. Naomi was thrilled at the prospect of a pleasant distraction from the darkness and sat up, with Eloise's help in plumping the down pillows behind her.

"Quick, Eloise, check the seal. Is there a small heart printed there?"

"Yes, Mum. It has an 'x' inside of it."

"Wonderful, Allison is fine," Naomi sighed. "You see, ever since we received the letter from Paris, announcing that Edward had passed on, Allison and I have been a bit leery of opening mail. When Allison attended school in Germany, we created a code. If the post bore a stamped heart, it contained good news; if the content was despairing, the absence of the heart forewarned the reader. However, after one incident when Allison inadvertently forgot to use the stamp, I nearly had heart failure, expecting the worst. Excuse the pun. That's when we agreed to stamp our correspondence with a heart encompassing an 'x' for good news, one without for bad."

"It's beyond me, Mum," Eloise smiled and proceeded to read Allison's letter.

"Dearest Mummy,

I have the most wonderful news! I met a charming gentleman, at a small restaurant in London Square. His name is Jackson Rands. We found one another so agreeable, that we have scarcely spent a moment of our days apart.

Yesterday, he surprised me with the adorable boiled wool jacket that I was admiring, while we were window-shopping at Selfridges's on Oxford, last week. Mummy, it has a zipper! One must keep abreast of the times! I'm certain I will be mistaken for a sophisticated lady of twenty-five, at the very least, when I'm wearing it!

You cannot possibly guess, to which event I will be attending with this handsome escort. Being the mystery lover that you are, I will give you a hint: it will take place in Germany. Enough games! Jack is taking me to the celebration for Bruno Walter, the new director of the Munich Opera! I am thrilled, as you can imagine, to be returning to Germany, much less to be rubbing elbows with any number of Germany's acclaimed thirty-thousand millionaires.

No, I have not forgotten that "money isn't everything." You will be proud to know, that I have not so much as hinted an inquiry to Jack's financial state. He does not put on airs of a wealthy man, but seems to be monetarily secure.

I must say that Jack is a tad socially reserved, directing his primary attention to me, but schedules numerable engagements for us. In our spare time, I have been instructing him in foxtrot lessons. We practice for an hour, nearly every day, in preparation for the grand gala. We are quite a pair on the ballroom floor; though we are no match for Irene and Vernon Castle, as yet.

I just finished reading D.H. Lawrence's *The White Peacock*. Have you started the copy of his latest, *The Trespasser* that I sent to you? Jack's favorite author is the American, Jack London. Isn't it amusing, that my Jack in London prefers Jack London?

I guess my giddiness is apparent, as it is 12:20 p.m. I am yawning uncontrollably now, and Jack and I have a full day ahead of us. He will be picking me up at my flat, at 9'oclock tomorrow morning. We are placating the youth within, by going to see the statue of "Peter Pan" in Kensington Gardens and then, we are off to the cinema, after breakfast in the square.

Give my regards to the Zigmanns and a kiss to Patience. I hope your journey was a successful one. Speaking of, or should I say "writing of," journeys, I was sorry to receive the news of Claudia's aunt, lost on the Titanic last year. We will all miss her laughter and compassionate nature. God Bless you Mummy, I miss you greatly. Hopefully, Jack and I can schedule a visit with you in the next couple of months. I think that you will adore him!

Your Baby, Allison."

"Thank you Eloise. Isn't that just grand? Allison has a companion. He sounds perfect for her, doesn't he?"

"Yes, Mum. She seems to be enjoying herself in London. I wish that you would have given me permission to notify her about your accident. But now, you need to go to sleep, so that you can take in a nap, before Dr. Lambert arrives," Eloise insisted.

Later that day, the doctor entered the McDonnally home, at a quarter past three, to remove Naomi's bandages and to make a final check of her overall condition. Aside from a few, slow healing bruises, she was given a clean bill of health and warned to avoid anymore "apples and pears," cat-stairs, combinations.

Eloise was pleased to get back to her normal routine, leaving Naomi to get reacquainted with Patience and to enjoy the privacy of the master bedroom. Naomi's first priority was to kneel and give thanks for being one of the sighted members of the world and for her wonderful caregivers. Surveying the room for the first time, in what seemed an eternity, she felt a shiver of guilt, with the seemingly, irreconcilable dispute with Hiram, nagging, relentlessly, at her peace-seeking conscience.

I really shouldn't have taken up residency here, she thought as she admired the velvet furnishings and embossed wall covering.

This is Hiram's home now and after our last encounter, I am sure that he will be back to reclaim it and to send me on my way, back to London. With thoughts of the cottage, her home with Allison for the past eighteen years, she lifted her daughter's letter from the dressing table and held it to her lips. She noticed a scent of lavender from the envelope, then, she took another sniff; the scent was a familiar one.

The last time that I enjoyed the fragrance of lavender was on my sixteenth birthday. It was my favorite. Hiram gave me my first bottle of perfume. Pity I had to leave it at Grimwald. Without another thought, she kissed the treasured correspondence and placed it in her bag, sitting by the window. Scanning the room for her shawl, she noticed a small, emerald green glass vase of forget-me-nots on the top shelf of the tall, narrow bookcase, next to the window.

"What's this Payshe?" she asked her friend, squinting curiously, from the dressing table bench. She lifted the vase from the shelf and studied the delicate petals of the bouquet, spotting a tiny scroll between the stems. She plucked the rolled paper from the flowers and giving her mischievous pet a second look, she reconsidered her placement of the vase on the dressing table and returned it to the shelf, out of harms way. Naomi inquisitively unrolled the paper and read silently:

Seeing is believing, Naomi.
        Lucas McClurry

She reread the note and conferred with her little friend, now balancing itself on its hind legs, with an outstretched front leg, pawing at the curled paper.

"What does it mean, Patience?" *Whatever the implications, it has a hopeful ring to it.* Naomi carefully manipulated the paper, returning it appropriately to the vase.

She turned to the window and smiled down on the grounds below, where a handful of the flowers, that Eloise had planted, were blooming, but did little to enhance the enormous garden. Naomi appreciated the specks of color, having lived in total darkness. She inadvertently, imagined the author of the note waving up at her. She stood, smiling peacefully, for several minutes, enjoying the view, knowing that, unfortunately, autumn was eminent and the garden would soon return to its hibernating state, hidden beneath a coverlet of fallen oak leaves.

Arianna Snow

Chapter V

"The Woods"

"Should ye see, afar off,
that worth winning,
Set out on the journey
with trust;
And ne'er heed if your path
at beginning
Should be among brambles
and dust."

— Eliza Cook

Naomi ventured downstairs for the first time, taking care to hold the handrail. Her first supper with the Zigmanns, since the accident, began with colcannon (meatballs in broth and an assortment of vegetables in butter) and ended with Eloise's moist dark gingerbread. Naomi spent the remainder of the evening in the study, engaged in a serious game of chess with Mr. Zigmann. Albert's expertly prepared peat fire kept the September chill at bay, crackling merrily in the oversized fireplace, while the four, Patience included, enjoyed the early autumn atmosphere.

Eloise continued with her knitting, battling with Patience over the ball of yarn, until Naomi drank her last sip of tea and victoriously announced, "Checkmate!" Albert shook his head in defeat, protesting that Naomi's chats with his wife, during his turns, had broken his concentration. Eloise retaliated with a snicker, rolled up her knitting, placed it in the basket and leaned back to rest her tired eyes. Together the opponents placed the ivory pieces back in the hinged walnut chest. When the last pawn was secure Mr. Zigmann gently placed the woolen shawl around his wife's shoulders for their return to the cottage. Naomi offered to join them on their walk to the back gate. She put on the navy fisherman's knit cardigan which Allison had sent to her from Munich several years earlier. Naomi was certain that even the short jaunt to the cottage would be a refreshing change from the confinement she had endured.

The three left by way of the pantry door, leaving Naomi's pet to the comfort of the basket by the fire. Eloise had prepared the little cat bed in hopes of deterring Patience from planting itself on her lap. However, Naomi often reminded the frustrated maid that there is something to be said about cats being attracted to those who do not appreciate their presence. Patience took refuge in her basket, only when she detected that Eloise was leaving indefinitely, much to the maid's chagrin.

As Naomi bid the Zigmanns goodnight, standing alone in the garden, she noticed lights appearing at Brachney Hall. Her curiosity with the generous neighbor, led her to take a closer look, but once beyond the fountain she began to have second thoughts about the endeavor. A clearer view of the neighbor's home would demand traversing the oak forest, adjoining the grounds.

She had been uncomfortable in the woods after dark, since a small child of six years, when she had become lost in the pine windbreak, at her uncle's farm in Edinburgh. At fifteen, Naomi had chosen to use the forest between the estates as her topic for a descriptive oral essay assignment. This was gradually restored to her memory, as she approached the foreboding oaks.

"The unearthly shadows of the leering forest appeared with the dreaded onset of yet another uninvited dusk. They lay silently, triggering a discomforting sense of unwelcome visitors on the desolate grounds," she recited dramatically, making her way into the woods.

She began with caution and once enclosed by the mammoth hardwoods, her pace quickened, until someone speaking her name, startled her. She was relieved, but a little nervous, in recognizing it to be the Voice of Lucas McClurry.

"Oh, hello, Mr. McClurry. You frightened me; I wasn't expecting to see anyone out here tonight."

"I'm just thankful that you can see!" he remarked cheerfully.

"Yes sir, I am, as well. May I take this opportunity to extend my gratitude for the time and care you devoted to me, and oh, yes, for the lovely bouquet."

"The pleasure was all mine."

"Well, I cannot thank you enough. It would have been a tremendous burden on Mrs. Zigmann, without you."

Naomi, now comforted by the fact that the scar, previously hidden by the bandages, remained concealed in the shadows.

"Where are you headed Mrs. McDonnally?" he asked from the blackness. Naomi took a second to answer, somewhat embarrassed, but trying to be truthful.

"I saw your lights go on and I—" she stammered.

"So you were planning to visit me."

"I believe so," she admitted, feeling like a small child caught with her hand in the biscuit jar.

Stepping closer, he questioned, "Has the master of the manor returned?"

The unexpected query silenced Naomi. After a brief pause, she answered, "Not yet. Soon, hopefully," she said in a rather melancholy tone, dropping her head, feeling shamefully responsible. The Master of Brachney Hall moved slowly through the shadows toward her and carefully lifted her chin gently with his fingertips.

"Patience, my dear," he spoke softly. Turning, he disappeared with the sound of his footsteps dissipating into the darkness that sealed around him. The tenderness of his voice, the manner in which he spoke, it all came fleeting back—the confusion, the Voice without a face.

But it's impossible, she thought, as his name flowed silently through her lips, *Edward?* The realization was overpowering, she could not hold back.

"Edward!! ...Edward!!" she screamed frantically and started running toward the direction of his departure. She ducked beneath branches, trying desperately to move forward with or without the aid of a path to reach him. Breathless, she stopped, and attempted to make one more, desperate call, when a hand from the darkness behind her, muffled it. Before Naomi had a chance to panic, the red-bearded man slowly removed his hand from her mouth, turned her around, peered into her anxious green eyes, and spoke.

"Yes, Naomi." She stood trembling, breathing deeply, with a firm grip on the wrist of the hand that had silenced her. She stared at the not so familiar face, trying to mentally shave away the beard, which the Edward she had known, had never worn.

"It can't be you, it just can't..."she whispered and closed her eyes, fainting into his arms. Edward lifted her limp body and held her close then carried her to the safety of his home on the hill, with a *deja vous* of the journey to the doctor, so many years ago.

Naomi awoke on Edward's sofa, dazed and unaware of her surroundings, her head swimming with questions. Within seconds, her eyes were fixed on the ghost of a man who had always taken care of her. He sat, smiling, next to her, waiting for her to collect her thoughts, so that he could proceed in explaining his presence. Her reaction in seeing Lucas McClurry transform into Edward McDonnally was again one of disbelief; but gradually, she accepted the reality of his being. Once she escaped the dream state, she fell to tears of joy and wept with her dear friend and benefactor.

After a long comforting embrace, Edward suggested that the reunited couple sit by the pond, and enjoy the evening breeze. Mutual consent sent them strolling hand-in-hand down to the wrought iron bench by the water's edge, where they discussed his miraculous return from the dead, under a billion stars.

"As cliché as it may sound, due to circumstances beyond my control, it was necessary that I fake my death and take on a new identity. I had word sent to the Moor News, of my supposed death, and had my obituary printed, leaving the manor to Hiram, the rightful heir. Having made several attempts over the years to locate him, I relied on the news of my alleged death, and the McDonnally clan's notoriety, to inform all of Britain and Europe, as well."

"Edward, you faked your death, just to bring Hiram home?!"

"In part, Naomi."

"In part?"

"Honestly, I would like to share the details with you, but as yet, I can't. However, I can assure you, that I was not being pursued by Scotland Yard... not as yet; there are laws about faking your own death... The Zigmanns were to continue their employ at the manor until Hiram returned to claim his inheritance. If and when he arrived in Lochmoor, Eloise was instructed to relay the information to you, giving you the opportunity to reconcile; something I know that you have been praying for all these years. All you need to know is that my stay at Brachney Hall is a temporary one. I bought Brachney Hall under, the assumed name to keep a watchful eye on the manor... Once all is well, I will sell Brachney Hall and move on, and leave you and Hiram to the life together that you have been deprived of."

His elusive answers were more than Naomi could bear. However, she felt that any further intrusion into his private life would be unconscionable, considering his benevolence with her and her daughter.

"The Zigmanns know that you're not..." she hesitated, feeling understandably betrayed.

"Please do not blame them. They were sworn to secrecy, allowing me to have the opportunity to reveal my identity, when I saw fit."

Naomi graciously changed the subject. "I left London immediately with Eloise's news. As it stands, my meetings with Hiram have been anything, but pleasant and I'm beginning to lose faith in the relationship. Hiram doesn't seem to have any intention of forgiving me, much less a desire for reconciliation. I don't know what more I can say to him, Edward."

Edward reached down, took her hand in his, and sympathetically suggested, "Tell him that you love him."

Those were strange words, Naomi thought, coming from a man who spoke only once of her relationship with Hiram— the day he gave her

Patience, the tiny kitten that he pulled magically from his coat pocket. Naomi raised her eyebrows and grinned skeptically, with no comment.

Edward walked Naomi back to the manor and reluctantly ended his evening with her. He avoided the issue of the "circumstances beyond his control" that he had mentioned. He walked away guilty, aware that this was not the only information that he was withholding from his wife, in name only.

The red-bearded man is dear Edward, she thought, as she watched him heading back, with his new name, to his new home. Naomi entered the hall and returned to the parlor to snuff the lamps. She reflected on the innocent greeting from the window, the hours that Edward sat anonymously by her side and his recent unsolicited advice.

What other possible reasons could he have had to go to such lengths to force him to change his identity?

"He's truly amazing.... thank you, God, for bringing him back into my life," she whispered reverently as she climbed the stairs to the master bedroom.

Any ill feelings, toward Eloise quickly dissipated, when Naomi found the room in good order with the bed neatly turned down and her clothing pressed, ready for the next day. Eloise had been a good friend to her and a trustworthy employee to Edward. She sat down at the dressing table and unclipped the barrette from her hair, when she noticed that she had failed to return the contents of the wooden box. She carried it downstairs to the parlor table, returned it, and then stepped over to admire the reconstructed, freshly grouted hearth tiles, a welcomed embellishment to the antique fireplace.

Mr. Zigmann's repair is quite professional. She felt certain that no one would ever suspect the conflict, which took place there, a month ago.

She hurried back upstairs to enjoy the luxury of the large bath and prepared for bed. She lifted the hem of the soft cotton gown that hung loosely down to her ankles and knelt to say a special prayer for Edward, fearing that he was still in grave danger; a deduction stemming from delving into umpteen mystery cases. Before rising, she bit her lip, and included another prayer for Hiram. She climbed in between the crisp white sheets and tucked Patience in beside her. Lifting Allison's picture from the nightstand, she pressed a kiss against the glass. She recited a scripture for her sweet daughter and her new beau, blew out the lantern, pulled the covers over her shoulders and reviewed her indecisive feelings for Hiram and Edward's unexpected suggestion: *Tell him that you love him.*

Her eyes were drawn to the bouquet of forget-me-nots sitting alone on the shelf, illuminated by the moonbeams piercing the window.

Seeing is believing. Lucas McClurry, indeed! All the same, Naomi had grown very fond of the little gift and found its presence in the bookcase, directly facing the foot of the bed, a comfort. It was the first thing which she saw when she awoke and the last before she closed her eyes each night. Although barely noticeable, in the massive room, the tiny flowers brought a speck of hope to a future of unknowns.

Arianna Snow

Chapter VI

"The Avenger"

"Truants from love,
we dream of wrath —
Oh, rather let us
trust the more!
Through all the wanderings
of the path,
We still can see
Our Father's door!!"

— Oliver Wendall Holmes

While hoping for Hiram's return, Naomi spent the next few weeks helping Eloise rejuvenate the early autumn garden, playing croquet, corresponding with Allison and strolling with Edward. She discontinued the chess tournament with Mr. Zigmann, due to Mr. Zigmann's claims that he was behind in his reading and did not have time for the "frivolity of silly games"; the final score being eight to three, her favor.

Naomi enjoyed sharing her daughter's delightful letters with Edward. The proud "parents" were equally curious about Allison's new companion and looking forward to meeting him in the upcoming weeks.

On the other hand, Naomi found Hiram's prolonged absence, not only disturbing, but also severely detrimental to the relationship for which she strived. Now, patience was a virtue that she was losing sight of with each day that passed. She finally relented in choosing not to dwell on the unlikely prospects of their reunion. She had comfortably settled in at McDonnally Manor, feeling quite at home, at this temporary home, away from home, in the company of Edward and the Zigmanns.

"Home" for Naomi had changed with the chapters of her life. As a child, she had left Grimwald and had moved to Newcastle with her mother, Beatrice Smithfield, after her abusive father, Nathan, had agreed to the divorce. With a series of threats and the heartbreaking stipulation that Beatrice consent to leave behind her newborn son, Jeremiah, Naomi's mother, battered and fearful for her daughter's safety, took her two-year-old daughter to the residence of the Landseer family. There, Beatrice took the position as a live-in-maid. Mother and daughter had lived there peaceably for ten years, until one evening when Naomi's mother failed to return home from a trip to the village mercantile. With Beatrice's accredited reputation as a doting, responsible parent and excellent servant, foul play was suspected. An extensive search, lasting nearly a fortnight, was unsuccessful in discovering any leads to her strange disappearance.

With Beatrice's absence, the authorities returned Naomi to Grimwald, at the tender age of twelve, where, she fearfully joined her brother, to live in the care of her despot father. Her newfound relationship with Hiram had been the only positive outcome of her return, as her brother, like their father, had become cruel and mean-spirited. Since her marriage to Edward, Naomi had only visited with her brother, Jeremiah, twice and left her father to his vices. Fortunately, Jeremiah later saw the error in his ways and matured into a responsible businessman.

Naomi was unaware that her father, Nathan, had combed all of Europe, searching for Edward with the relentless persistence of his Highlander forefathers, vengefully driven for years by the memory of Edward's assault on him and the dissolution of his despicable plan. Edward had remained in hiding, and out of Nathan's reach, until he could set up a trust fund to protect Naomi and Allison's financial security. Later, with the assistance of his dear friend Desilama Rahelaka, Naomi's husband staged his illness and death. Upon learning of Edward's passing in Paris, Nathan finally ended his search in Stockholm, where he met and married a

Swedish woman named Dagmar Arnoldson, a widow with three adult children. Dagmar had agreed to their betrothal, with the provision that she could return annually to visit her sons, Omar and Olaf, lumberjacks in Norway, and her only daughter, Gretchen, a bookkeeper at a woolen mill in Stockholm. Dagmar's only grandson, Andrej, Omar's son, was a bit of a rascal for a child of ten, but respected his grandmother. Nathan frequently threatened to straighten out the young scallywag, if given the opportunity to spend a week with a rod and the young mischief-maker.

Nathan brought Dagmar to Scotland to live at Grimwald. There, having spent several years as a clerk for a milliner in Sweden, she took employment at a local shop. Dagmar was a large, strong-willed, boisterous woman with a solid work ethic, an over-bearing countenance and was known to stand her ground with her husband. Ignorant of the strained father-daughter relationship, being a family ori-ented woman, she was displeased with the fact that she had not made the acquaintance of her step-daughter, Naomi. She vowed to rectify her situation after overhearing customers, at the shop, discuss-ing the estranged stepdaughter's visit to Lochmoor's McDonnally Manor.

With the added rumor that Naomi was wait-ing for Hiram to return, Nathan was more than happy to abide by Dagmar's wishes, to be driven to the manor. He secretly savored the thought of reviv-ing his first plan of action to regain possession of the estate, which he still maintained was rightfully his. As next of kin, he thought, if by chance, his widowed daughter were to finally marry Hiram, the unexpected disappearance of the wedded couple, would end his struggle to seize the property. However, he had no knowledge of the existence of the missing link to the line of heirs to McDonnally Manor, his adopted granddaughter, Allison Beatrice O'Connor. Dagmar, oblivious to her husband's treachery, planned to visit her stepdaughter at the end of the week.

After several impatient raps of the lion-headed doorknocker on that late September afternoon, Eloise opened the door to the front entrance of the manor house. The visiting pair introduced themselves and then with Nathan's insistence invited themselves into the McDonnally home, despite Eloise's reserved hesitation and half dozen excuses. Mr. and Mrs. MacKenzie seated themselves in the parlor to wait for the announcement of their arrival, scrupulously examining the furnishings. Nathan picked up the Polish carved box, glanced at its contents, sneered, and tossed it back on the table.

"Vat a beautiful hardt," Dagmar admired Albert's refurbishment. "And de carpet, it vill vear like iron," she remarked, running her fingers through the fibers. Nathan, scowling disdainfully at the portrait of Hiram's father ignored his wife's commentary, momentarily, then agreed, "Aye...aye," he imagined sitting in the overstuffed chair, smoking his pipe as new Master of McDonnally Manor.

In the meantime, Eloise had scurried across the hall to open the doors of the study, to inform Naomi of the unexpected guests. Naomi was engaged in her first game of cribbage, at the small marble table, with her worthy opponent, Edward. The shocking news of Nathan and Dagmar's arrival sent Edward to his feet in a split second. Dropping his playing cards to the floor, astonished to hear that his greatest adversary was across the hall, Edward fearfully announced, just above a whisper, "He can't find me here!" Both women, seeing his panic, realized the seriousness of the situation. Eloise pulled the doors to the study closed and quickly locked them. She began to weep in the hem of her apron, shaken with remorse for her inability to deter the intruders' entry. Naomi immediately sought to comfort her, and then turned to Edward, who was trying desperately to open the double hung window.

"It's no use," Eloise whispered between snifffles, "the ropes are broken." Naomi rushed to Edward's side.

"Edward, I'm sure that Nathan's forgotten that entire incident. Calm down," Naomi reassured. A loud banging at the study's pocket doors and her father's brash voice sent their hearts racing.

"Is this the way you treat your guests?!"

"Edward, it's been years, maybe he won't recognize you, he believes that you are dead," Naomi quickly rationalized, with a hushed tone.

"I will be, if he finds me here! He's been trailing me for years!"

"My father?! Is he the reason that you changed your identity?" her volume had increased with noted anger. "I'll tell them to leave!"

"No, Naomi, it's too late, you'll have to open the doors to talk to them," Edward conceded nervously.

Naomi scanned the room quickly, and then grasped Edward's hand and the tall wooden stool by the bookcase of leather bound classics.

"Make haste, get in there," Naomi instructed, pointing at the fireplace, "and stand on this stool!"

"What?! Are you touched in the head?!" Edward retorted softly.

"Just get in there quickly," Naomi demanded, shoving the stool towards him. Edward crawled into the mammoth fireplace and carefully climbed on the tall stool, maintaining his balance with aid of the flu walls.

While standing hidden in the darkness, Edward muttered, "A trifle early for St. Nick, isn't it?" followed by a droll comment as to Naomi's ingenuity, and then thanked God for the unseasonably warm weather permitting the availability of the fireplace.

The next moment, Eloise slid the study doors open to reveal Naomi seated at the table, casually playing solitaire. Eloise apologized for the delay, welcoming them in and then nervously attempted to clear the cards away. While fumbling with the deck she invites them to a game of gin rummy, praying that they would not accept the offer. Edward nearly fell off the stool, in hearing the maid's invitation. Perturbed by the distasteful request, the MacKenzies fortunately declined. As Naomi rose to meet Dagmar, she focused on her new stepmother, curbing her anger and avoiding any acknowledgement of her father's presence.

"How do you do? I'm Naomi." She offered her hand to Dagmar, withholding any judgment based on the marriage to her unsavory father.

"Fine tank you. You may call me Dagmar." She replied in her Swedish cadence, and then shook her stepdaughter's hand with a forceful grip and a pleased smile. She glanced around the room, noticing the stool's unlikely position and inquired curiously.

"Vat's dat stool doing in de fireplace?" Edward's heart skipped a beat.

Naomi turned to Eloise, searching for an answer, then retorted, "Eloise, did Mr. Zigmann fail to return the stool to the pantry after inspecting the flu, again?!" Eloise, as honest as her interrogator, denied the accusation with, "I don't think so Mum..."

Naomi pursed her lips trying to maintain the necessary expression, "After our guests leave, please inform Albert to return it to the pantry and I expect not another embarrassing incident such as this will occur."

"Yes, Mum!" Eloise saluted, going a bit overboard with her dutiful role. Naomi rolled her eyes and frowned slightly, although amused with her friend's exuberant response. The statuesque occupant of the green, wooden stool took a breath of relief; Dagmar appeared to be satisfied with the explanation.

"Aren't you going to address your father?" Nathan attempted to unnerve his daughter with the stern reprimand.

"Yes, vy dun't you vant to speak to yur foder? Dagmar questioned.

Naomi flinched slightly and bravely replied with simply, "Not at this time. Now, if you'll excuse us, I have another engagement," Naomi said coolly, left the study and then brushed passed them into the hall.

"Natan, vy vun't yur daughter speak to you?" the confused wife inquired, grabbing her husband's arm. Nathan responded with a low growl.

Naomi turned to her stepmother, "Dagmar, it was nice meeting you. My brother, Jeremiah, has spoken highly of you and the great improvements that you have made to Grimwald."

Dagmar thanked the hostess, while her husband, quite incensed by Naomi's inhospitable manner toward him, led the way to the door in a huff. With a wicked grin and a promise to return, he sent chills through his daughter. Eloise shuttled the undesirable guest and his interrogating wife through the hall with Naomi following close behind. Eloise opened the door, to find the portal brightened by the jovial face of Harriet Dugan, a short, stout, fiery red head in her mid-fifties.

"How do ye do, mum? I hope I willna be intrudin'," Harriet curiously remarked, surprised to see the couple, blocking the doorway.

"Mrs. Dugan, it's no trouble, come on in, they are just leaving," Naomi assured, relieved by the neighbor's perfect timing.

"Glad to see ye feelin' chipper, Mum. I'm sorry I couldna help me dear friend in the carin' for ye, but I'd promised Maryanne Wheaton, to look after the bairn. She was expectin' ye know. Oh, I canna tell you the difficulties the poor woman was havin', before she brought that wee lass into the world," Harriet raised her empty hand beckoning the heavens as she spoke.

The MacKenzies pushed their way, through the doorway to their carriage, past the chattering neighbor.

"Wee lass she was, too. Thank heavens; she and the babe are fine. Aye, speakin of Maryanne, I'm off to see her now, Good day! Oh..." Mrs. Dugan handed a brown paper package to Eloise. "Jon Wiggins sent these pickled pig's feet along wi' me for ye Eloise. I know how Mr. Zigmann delights over 'em."

"Thank you, you're an angel! Beautiful bonnet, Harriet!" Eloise called after her friend now waving, as she scurried down the cobblestone road. Naomi drew a deep breath and bolted the door without further delay.

With Harriet's departure, Naomi and Eloise ran to rescue Edward from the sooty sanctuary. Unfortunately, he came out looking quite differently from the way he appeared, prior to this venture. After considerable laughter, at Edward's expense, the three allies spent the next half hour, brushing the carbon and ashes from his hair, to restore it to its original condition. Edward's clothing was yet another matter. The two women insisted that he not move another inch, for fear he would soil the carpets. Their remedy for Edward, to don a pair of Albert's work trousers, his pinstriped cotton shirt and braces, led Edward to believe that the women were in cahoots for further merriment, in seeing him lost in apparel, nearly three sizes to large.

After changing into Mr. Zigmann's clothes, Edward discovered that he was correct in his prediction, when he met with the giddy conspirators returning to the study.

"Lose a little weight, Edward?" Naomi teased.

"You are certainly seaworthy. You come with your own set of sails!" Eloise giggled. Edward glanced up from adjusting his braces, to shoot a fabricated glare at the now hysterical women, bombarding him with the less than cricket phrases.

"Why you look like you couldn't kick the skin off a rice pudding!" Naomi blurted at the poor soul. While the two women were laughing uncontrollably,

Edward stood, resembling your typical clown, with his hands planted defiantly on his hips, shaking his cocked head of ruffled hair.

"I am so pleased to see you two ladies enjoying yourselves, maybe you would like me to perform some tricks for you," Edward grinned sarcastically. Naomi and Eloise, now snickering, strewn over the furniture, exhausted from their humoring frenzy, jumped to their feet, clutched hands, leaned toward their entertainer and proceeded to fervently sing what they considered the perfect childhood ditty.

"Take me to the circus, to see the funny clown. His hair looks like a porcupine; his nose is big and round!" Edward slumped hopelessly into the nearest chair, resting his head in his hands; half smiling, knowing that he was hopelessly at their mercy. The two women cheered, danced and around the study like schoolgirls, thoroughly pleased with their display.

That evening, Naomi and "Albert's comical twin" joined the Zigmanns for haggis (minced mutton, oatmeal, and spices boiled in sheep's stomach) with stovies (sides of potatoes cooked with onions), asparagus and assorted commentaries on their performances with the unwelcome visitors. After their meal, Naomi and Edward resumed their game of cribbage, with Naomi triumphant. Naomi quizzically doubted her opponent, who blamed his cramped encounter with the chimney and extraordinary volumes of soot, lining his lungs, for his less than perfect game strategy. Naomi turned and smiled at Albert, familiar with creative defense for a loss. The veteran loser smiled and patted Edward on the back, "It's no use McClurry, nice try anyway."

"Yes, that's right! You try maintaining two separate identities. It's a wonder, that I can do any-thing correctly," Edward, made one last pathetic ditch effort to justify his failure to win.

"You men just can't accept defeat to a woman. Excuse me, while I fetch sweets to cele-brate Mrs. McDonnally's victory," Eloise deduced. Naomi, with a tight-lipped smile, shrugged inno-cently, and placed the cards back in the package. Eloise left to the kitchen and returned promptly with a loaded serving tray.

"I have special afters, date bars and cus-tard," she invited. The four enjoyed the sweets, then retired for an evening of music and dance with Al-bert's first class fiddling accompaniment of jigs, reels, and polkas. Naomi, regretting having never learned to play an instrument, had a special admi-ration for Albert's accomplished musical talent. Be-fore Edward returned to Brachney Hall, he had the unpleasant task of informing Naomi that their days together were drawing to a close, for he would be taking a temporary leave to London on business. This trip would dually serve to prevent any further, near misses with her deplorable father.

"I'll be back my dear friend and until then, enjoy the remainder of your visit with future suc-cess and remember when conversing with others, that Edward McDonnally is no longer among the living." Naomi remained silent as they hugged and watched woefully after him, until he disappeared into the woods.

Chapter VII

"The Guest"

"And 'somebody's mother'
bowed low her head
In her home that night,
and the prayer she said
Was 'God be kind to the noble boy,
Who is somebody's son, and
pride and joy!"

—— Mary Dow Brine

Eloise spent the late autumn afternoon cultivating the flowerbeds and planting the complimentary, hyacinth bulbs from Mrs. Dugan, while Naomi sat, nearby, absorbed in the copy of *The Trespasser.* Covered with the quilt from the maid's room, Naomi seated in a white wicker chair, folded the page corner, to mark her place. She invited the busy gardener to hear the letter, which she received from Allison that morning. Eloise was delighted and sat back relaxing, propped on her gloved hands, with her legs extended before her, while Naomi removed the letter from the jacket of the book, unfolded it and began to read with maternal pride.

"Dearest Mummy,

How are you feeling? I hope you have fully recovered from your tumble with our favorite feline. I so wish that you had allowed me to join Eloise in caring for you! Please thank her for me, for her Excellence in nursing.

I have been caught in a whirlwind of social engagements with Jack and loving every minute of it! If all goes according to schedule, we will be visiting you in mid-October.

Thank your lucky stars that your daughter is still enjoying perfect health. On the way to the theatre, we ran into a little sticky wicket. It was none other than a Suffragette demonstration! Three cheers for Mrs. Pankhurst! We need more tough spirited women like her!

A bit of warning, if you don't recognize me, I'll be the lovely young woman with a head full of blonde curls! Yes, I took the leap and subjected myself to one of those new "permanent waves" to give my stribbly tresses a lift.

However, the results were hardly comparable to my mother's gorgeous auburn locks!

Well, have to beetle off, Love. I need to recheck my coiffure before Jack arrives. I hope my new appearance pleases him.

Yesterday, we went to the last cricket match of the season, on the village green in Dover, and tonight, we are going to Kent, to dine in Canterbury and then to tour the cathedral.

Take Care and Sweet Kisses
Mummy,
God bless you!

Your Social Princess,
Allison

P.S. Did you hear that Leo's "Mona" was found in Italy! Remember how disappointed I was when I traveled to the Louvre , a few years ago, and found it had been stolen? Maybe I can convince Mr. Rands to accompany me to Paris, to see it this spring!"

Eloise smiled while Naomi placed the letter back in the book, "Wonderful news, Mum! It will be a pleasant change, having a bit of youth at the manor, again. Do you think that I need one of those permanent waves?" Eloise asked with a sophisticated tone and a soiled, gloved hand framing her profile.

Naomi laughed, "No! You're beautiful just the way you are," playfully pulling the brim of the gardener's sunbonnet down over Eloise's face.

"Join me in a spot of tea, Eloise?"

"Most certainly, Mum," Eloise rose to her feet with the aid of Naomi's hand, gladdened by the prospect of escaping the heat, to enjoy a retreat from her horticultural duties. Eloise followed Naomi to the kitchen, methodically stretching each limb to remove the kinks of older age.

Eloise began stoking the stove, when sudden erratic rapping at the front entrance unnerved Naomi, now juggling the fine china teacups, which she lifted from the breakfront. Knowing that Mr. Zigmann was busy mending the fence at the cottage, the apprehensive women simultaneously exchanged worried glances, fearing that Nathan, Naomi's deranged father, had kept his promise to return. Naomi gently placed the cups on the blue gingham tablecloth and considered the possibility, that the caller may in fact, be the scornful returning Master Hiram.

Naomi motioned to Eloise, armed with a stick of wood. The shaken women now moved in unison, step by step, through the entry hall, with the common reluctance that London women shared, since the terror of the infamous Jack the Ripper in '88. Eloise peered out the sidelight, but failed to catch a glimpse of the visitor. With one last rap and an unexpected thud, the women slowly unlocked the door and cracked it open. The weight of the visitor's falling body against the door, forced it open. At first glance, it was obvious to the women, that it was a young male, who had suffered extensively at the hands of his aggressors. The victim lay in a crumpled heap, across the threshold, facedown in tattered, blood-stained apparel. Naomi gasped, as Eloise knelt down and turned the stranger's head.

Eloise shrieked, "Guillaume, my son!" Naomi was equally shocked, not expecting to meet the Zigmann progeny under these horrific conditions.

The desperate women struggled to turn the young man over, whose right shoulder was bleeding profusely. They loosened his clothing, and carefully drug his limp body to the center of the hall. Naomi snatched a pillow from the parlor and slipped it under his head, while his fearful mother lowered her head to his chest and surveyed his shallow breathing. Eloise begged Naomi to retrieve her husband, and then scrambled to the kitchen to light the stove to boil water.

Receiving the disturbing news of his son's return, Albert Zigmann tossed the hedge clippers to the ground and hurried into the manor house. Meanwhile, Naomi rushed to aid Eloise in recovering bandage materials from the storage shelves, under the stairs.

The Zigmanns carefully transported their son to the cot in the small maid's room, off the kitchen, where they bathed and wrapped Guillaume's wounds, then dressed him in one of his father's nightshirts from the cottage. His breathing improved, but he remained in a state of delirium, for several hours, from a severe blow to the head. His parents closely monitored his condition until he regained partial consciousness and fell into a deep peaceful sleep.

Naomi watched sympathetically and studied the face of the young man, not much older than her daughter. She wished that there was more that she could do to help; she knew that it was futile to try contacting Dr. Lambert, who was attending a seminar on new surgical procedures in Norwich. Naomi went to the kitchen to prepare a simple supper of yesterday's cullen skink (creamed potatoes and smoked haddock), Wensleydale cheese and hot cross buns. She invited the Zigmanns to share the informal meal at the kitchen table, where the three friends grasped hands, lowering their heads in prayer for the meal and recovery of the beloved son.

Naomi relieved Eloise and her husband, Albert, from their midnight watch, nursing the patient with cool applications to the goose egg bump on his forehead. Naomi grimaced vicariously, as Guillaume fought to endure the excruciating pain from the stab wound to his right shoulder. He was a stately looking gentleman despite his wounds, she observed, with his well-chiseled jaw line and prominent cheekbones that complimented his straight nose.

He reminds me of that young prince who I met in Paris. At least, he claimed to be one, she smiled and blotted the struggling victim's forehead with a damp compress. Guillaume began to stir with his dark lashes fluttering slightly and his eyelids slowly uncovering his deep blue eyes. Even in the candlelight, Naomi found clarity and brightness of color in the striking sapphires, now gazing up at her.

"How do you do?" Naomi welcomed the guest as he gradually regained consciousness.

"Bon Jour... Madame," he reciprocated with a perplexed glance at his new surroundings.

"If you please, where am I?" he spoke with some difficulty.

"McDonnally Manor, sir. I am Naomi McDonnally."

"Pleased to meet you, Madame, ...I'm...ahhh," a sharp pain in his shoulder prevented him from the introduction.

"No need to bother, I know who you are. Your parents are the caretakers here, Guillaume."

"McDonnally Manor...McDonnally Manor?" he repeated trying to restore some sense of order to his memory.   "Yes... I was en route to visit my parents when I was accosted by highwaymen. I guess, when they found my identification, they immediately assumed that I was French... the French are not, always well received you know. That's the last thing that I remember. I guess they got the best of me," he half-smiled.

"How are you feeling, Guillaume? Any headache?" Naomi asked politely, knowing his response.

"I feel as though a team of horses trampled me, followed by a brigade of motorcars," he replied, with as much humor as he could muster.

"I'm sorry, young man, but the best cure is waiting for you in the parlor. I must go now and tell your parents that you've come back to us!"

"Wait, Madame! Please tell me, how are my parents? Are they well?"

"Oh, they're wonderful; a bit distraught with worry over you, but physically fine."

"Thank you for your attentive care and please extend my gratitude to the master of the house, as well."

"I will... when I see him... he's not here presently."

Noting her troubled tone, Guillaume hastened her to his parents. Naomi excused herself and ran to the parlor, now a dormitory to the slumbering Zigmanns.

"Wake up, your son's awake and lucid. He's asking for you!" Naomi announced jubilantly. The Zigmanns found Guillaume alert and smiling at the sight of his misty-eyed parents.

Naomi withdrew, unnoticed, to the kitchen for a cup of tea, where she discovered Patience begging at the pie safe for a tasty morsel. Naomi found a small piece of salmon for her cat, poured her tea, and replaced the embroidered tea cozy, Amanda's handiwork. She sat down at the table, finding comfort in the nostalgic surroundings of the rural kitchen, frozen in time, void of the gaslights of London. She sipped the hot, cherished tea, then overpowered with exhaustion, drowsily returned to the parlor and snuggled under her shawl on the divan. Patience faithfully joined her beloved owner, curling up at her feet, purring steadily. Naomi enjoyed a sense of blissful peace, witnessing the reunited family; a welcome sight, considering her relatively solitary life now, with Allison, Hiram, Edward, and Jeremiah away. The only family, within close proximity, was that of her infamous father and new stepmother.

After a short nap, Naomi made a final check on the Zigmann family and then made every effort to climb the long staircase with the snoozing cat in tow. After jotting a short note to her daughter, she moved Patience to the pillow next to hers and before the smoke from the dark lamp faded into the night, the old friends were sound asleep.

Albert and Eloise sat watching over their son in the twilight of the morning; their son improving with each hour, approaching dawn.

The Zigmanns, Albert and Eloise, had met in their early twenties and married, but were not blessed with a child until late in life. Guillaume, their miracle baby, was born to the couple in Paris, and named for Eloise's father, Guillaume Boyer. Later they moved to Scotland to assume their positions as caretakers at McDonnally Manor, while Guillaume attended school in Paris. When their son graduated, his future in architecture led him to London, presenting the opportunity for a visit with his parents.

The strenuousness of the prior evening brought reposeful sleep to Naomi until midmorning. She awoke smiling, envisioning Eloise gently stroking her son's soft brown, wavy hair, as only a loving mother could.   Naomi counted her blessings for having a daughter in good health. Then Naomi bathed and donned her favorite plaid skirt and ivory lace blouse, before slipping on her stockings and black leather boots. She lifted her coin purse, from her bag, and tucked it into her skirt pocket, then took a couple minutes to tease her feline friend with the hairbrush. Patience, wiggled on its back, pawing playfully, until Naomi headed for the door. Her cat sat up with perked ears and listened to the final instructions to keep out of mischief.

Naomi rushed down the maid's stairs and tiptoed through the pantry to take a peek in at McDonnally Manor's newest resident. To her dismay, she discovered that the cot was neatly prepared with fresh linen, with not the slightest trace of the young Zigmann. Naomi assumed that he had joined his parents in the cottage, until a small note, propped up against the sugar canister on the sideboard, caught her eye. Naomi read the explanation revealing that Eloise and Albert had driven their son to the physician in Gavonshire, several hours away; Naomi feared that Guillaume's condition may be worsening. However, she remained positive, having heard that Dr. Kelly's credentials were impeccable and his bedside manner unmatched.

Naomi, slipped the note into her skirt pocket, pulled on her sweater from the hook in the hall and ventured outside for a breath of fresh air to wait for the postman, to purchase a stamp for her note to Allison.

She admired the incredible improvement to the manor's façade, Mr. Zigmann's excellent job of painting the columns and tuck-pointing the brick wall. Brachney Hall stood looming in the distance, just beyond the woods, where she met Edward not so long ago. It appeared so remote and lonely to her now. Several minutes passed before the postman arrived on horseback to make his daily delivery.

"Grand weather, for this time of year, ay Mum?" Mr. Kilvert casually addressed Naomi, handing down two letters for the Zigmanns.

"Yes, Mr. Kilvert. How are Mrs. Kilvert and the children?" Naomi asked, examining the letters, with the minute hope of finding one addressed to her.

"Fine, thank ye, Mum. Jake will be takin' over the livery next week. He bought it from Mr. Leslie, retirin' ye know. Bad back. Nice havin' connections, bein' the postman."

"How proud you must be. Jake is very young to handle the livery alone. Why, he's only twenty-two or three."

"Aye, he'll be only twenty-four in December, but he's strong as an ox and has a head for business. He'll be needin' a good income. He and Agnes Murray are to be wed in the spring."

"Wee Agnes Murray! I haven't seen the lass since she was a babe! My how time gets away from you."

"Speakin' of time, I should be gettin' along, Mrs. McDonnally."

"Oh, I nearly forgot. I need to purchase a stamp, for a letter. I hope to write to my daughter, later today," she explained, pulling her coin purse from her pocket. Will Kilvert took the coins and handed her a stamp, tipped his hat and galloped off.

"Ye'll be gettin' an invitation to th' weddin'!"

"I'll be looking forward to it," Naomi called back, placing the stamp and letters in her pocket. She watched the chestnut horse pause at the Dugan's, imagining a grown up Agnes Murray dressed in a bridal gown. Then she remembered her wedding day.

I pray that their wedding day is more pleasant than mine was.

A young boy, of about thirteen, on a bright red bicycle broke her train of thought. The delivery boy paused to have her sign for a telegram, giving his apologies for the delay, which was due to an unexpected deluge of deliveries. She thanked him quickly with a few coins from her purse and bid him "good day." She found herself looking for the telltale heart on the back of the telegram, sighed, shook her head and proceeded to open it with nervous thoughts of her loved ones. Her eyes widened as she read the following:

MY DEAR NAOMI-

I HAVE NEWS OF HIRAM'S WHEREABOUTS. HE IS IN TOWN. WORD IS THAT HE IS NOT ALONE IN LONDON. HE HAS BEEN SEEN IN THE COMPANY OF THE SAME WOMAN ON COUNTLESS OCCASIONS. I FELT THAT YOU WERE ENTITLED TO THIS INFORMATION. I'M SORRY TO BE THE BEARER OF ILL-TIDINGS.

YOUR LOVING SERVANT, EDWARD

Naomi suffered conflicting emotions; her first compulsion to shred the message was foregone by the second reading. She felt her ties to Hiram being severed with each statement, but her temper mellowed as she caressed the words of Edward's chivalrous closing. Her eyes welled up with tears of regret, loss, guilt, and a tinge of relief, as she sat down on the small stonewall, where the sun shone warmly on her flushed cheeks. She wiped her eyes with the back of her sleeve, and then stared blankly at the rolling hills across the moors. The dampened correspondence slid through her trembling fingers to the ground, while the tiny red speck, of the fateful deliverer, moved down the distant road, and then vanished over a hill, carrying with him, hopes of a renewed love of eighteen years. Naomi sat motionless, stunned for several minutes strapped by pangs of revenge, restrained by Sarah's advice. A gust of wind tossed a lock of hair before her eyes, awakening her from her state of limbo.

"Well...what's done is done," she spoke aloud with false self-assurance. "I explained the situation to him and he chose not to forgive me. I had hoped that he..." her voice cracked and she began to sob with her face in her cupped hands.

Not a moment too soon, she heard the familiar Voice, "Dear Naomi," as a comforting arm embraced her. She looked up through her tears to see Edward's sympathetic eyes. She closed hers and reopened them, questioning *Could it be?* It was he; her dearest friend in the flesh, actually seated beside her. She turned and hugged him gratefully, in appreciation for his unparalleled savoir-faire.

He comforted her with soft-spoken words, "I knew the minute that I sent the telegram that it was a mistake. I am so sorry. I should have delivered the news personally. I left immediately, hoping to arrive before it was delivered."

Naomi said nothing but reached for his hand and numbly looked out across the estate. Edward looked down, with saddened eyes at their locked hands and then at her statuesque profile. Then, he too, sought solace in the rolling hills beyond. The couple sat silently, inanimate in the landscape, like models for an impressionist portrait in oil. Naomi was drained from months of the distressful, irreconcilable relationship with Hiram; Edward was equally despaired by his concealed feelings of love for her.

After a quarter hour, Edward broke the silence in a vibrant tone. "Enough tears, let's go, my lady!" He grasped her small, soft hands and lifted her to her feet. "We're going to enjoy the afternoon!" Naomi forced a smile and took his arm, then walked down the road, through the woods, to the home of this very special man, Brachney Hall.

Arianna Snow

Chapter VIII

"The Picnic"

"Let us, then, be up and doing,
With a heart for any fate;
Still achieving, still pursuing,
Learn to labor and to wait."

—Henry Wadsworth Longfellow

Naomi was curiously considering her companion's plans for the day, when they entered the beautiful, marbled entry hall of Edward's home.

"First my dear, 'tis nearly noon and I'll venture to guess that you had very little for breakfast. We need to replenish our energy to face this new day!" he reported. "Come with me and we will prepare a meal fit for a king, for an outing down by the pond."

Naomi watched in disbelief while Edward gathered several ingredients from the pantry, professionally analyzing a number of spices to prepare his favorite stew.

"I didn't know that you were an accomplished chef," she remarked with suspicion.

"There are a lot of things that you don't know about me, my lady. But in time, you might even learn to appreciate this old Jack of all trades," he laughed boastfully. The mere mention of the name "Jack" lifted her spirits, reminding her that she, like Allison should be enjoying life to the fullest.

"What I do know is that you're the best friend that a person could ever have," Naomi responded gratefully.

Edward blushed sheepishly and returned the compliment with, "And you my dear, are a breath of fresh air, a Godsend to any man that has the pleasure of making your acquaintance."

With Edward's compliment, Naomi's troubles seemed to descend, uplifting her body. She felt as light as a feather, scurrying around the kitchen, assisting the chef, gathering more ingredients for Edward's concoction. After adding the prunes, the connoisseurs began to question the actual maximum number of different ingredients, which one could include in a stew and have it still be what most people considered edible. The content of the large pot was swelling just below the rim, when they decided that their creative talents may have bubbled out of control. As the "best stew this side of the Thames" began to boil, bits of nuts, cabbage and tomato came to life, making a concerted effort to escape their fate as dinner for two. Before Edward had a chance to deter the escapees with a large metal lid, the incarcerating pot spit out another cup of fleeing prisoners to the adjacent wall, floor and stovetop.

Naomi teased the master chef, "Jack of all trades, master of none," wiping a few straggling inmates from her apron and blouse sleeve.

"Master of none! Hold your tongue, wench! How dare you speak to the Master of Brachney Hall in that manner!" Edward objected trying to maintain a serious expression.

"Master of Broccoli Hall, maybe," she chuckled, as she lifted a piece of green vegetation from his shoulder.

The culinary partners broke into laughter, exchanging a variety of derogatory comments on their cooking abilities, as they cleaned up remnants from the stew. They worked famously together, gathering foodstuffs including: fresh fruit, shortbread, Yorkshire pudding and vegetables to accompany the main entrée, now simmering on the stove. Edward poured the stew into a canister and placed it in the large woven basket from the West Indies, tucking an older linen tablecloth tightly around it. Naomi collected plates and cups from the cupboard and placed them gently on top.

Naomi left her feelings for Hiram, at the portal to McDonnally Manor and found herself, floating peaceably in the humor and gentleness of the husband, whom she never really knew.

They looked favorably toward the fair weather sky, when the protective Edward suggested, "Mind your step," as they followed the staggered, moss stained flagstones down to the pond, where he spread out the tablecloth on the grass near the swaying willow. Together, they arranged the feast, and then bowed their heads respectfully in grace.

"Today we offer our special gratitude for the wonderful bounty and blessed friendship," Edward spoke solemnly.

They finished most of their meal, save the main. Even with a sprinkle of salt and pepper, the gourmets made a unanimous decision, that the cuisine was not palatable for the human race. Naomi tossed some breadcrumbs to the ducks that abandoned the pond to join them. An annoyed Edward threatened, "Here you silly fowl, have some of this delicious stew.'"

"Leave them alone, Edward, I think they're delightful!" Naomi objected, thrilled by the birds comical campaign of non-stop debating over the leadership role.

Edward, feeling upstaged by the unrehearsed antics of the intruding, feathered comedians, successfully provided his own form of entertainment, juggling with two apples and a plum. Although his talents were next to nil, Naomi was delighted with his attempts and applauded fervently.

Edward then invited Naomi to search the clouds for familiar faces and animal forms. "Look over there, Naomi!"

"Where?"

"Over there!   It looks like Joseph Dugan's mule!"

"Where?"

"Up there. To the right."

"To the right of what, Edward?"

"See that oak?"

"Which oak?"

"That oak, about half mile away."

"Which oak? There are a dozen oaks."

"The oak with the nest?"

"Which nest? Oh, stop it, Edward!" Naomi playfully pushed him away. Edward snickered then continued in his defense.

"No really. See that clump of trees?"

"Yes..." Naomi rolled her eyes, scowling, trying to maintain a serious countenance.

"Now follow it straight up..." Edward instructed.

"There's nothing there, Edward."

"By George, it moved."

"Oh, Edward!"

"Now wait!   There it is! It's right above that white barn!"

"Edward... That is not a mule. If anything, it's a hare."

"Well, it used to be a mule," Edward insisted.

"Oh, Edward, how many hares have you known that used to be mules?" Naomi teased.

"I've seen mule hair," he interjected innocently.

"Oh, Edward!" Naomi stood up and dispersed the remaining breadcrumbs over her companion's head and shot straight away to the pond. Edward brushed aside the artillery and took out after the attractive enemy. When he caught up with her, he lifted her by the waist and spun her around in mid-air, which sent her to screaming and laughing. Out of breath and suffering from a mild case of vertigo, Edward gently landed Naomi on a flagstone by the water. The laughter ceased and silence fell uncomfortably between them. Edward's now serious eyes, left hers and fell to his hands at her waist. He removed them instantly and with a deep sigh, placed a secure arm over her shoulders; Naomi glanced up at him approvingly.

Edward led the stroll around the perimeter of the pond, informing Naomi of the various improvements that had been made in the last decades, followed by a thorough synopsis of the history of the estate. Dusk soon demanded that they pack up and return to the manor house. Their wonderful evening overshadowed any mention of the telegram.

With the lights burning in the manor cottage, Naomi, concerned with the state of Guillaume's health, and the two letters in her pocket, suggested that they visit the Zigmanns. Edward, delighted at the prospect of meeting the young Guillaume, escorted Naomi through the woods to the cottage, where Eloise welcomed her guests, pleased to see the Master of Brachney Hall, safe and sound. Naomi and Edward found Guillaume, sipping hot barley soup, while resting in the rocking chair with his feet supported by a needlepoint footstool. His smile broadened, upon meeting Edward and suggested that the guest sit next to him, so they could get better acquainted.

Eloise happily reported, "Dr. Kelly said that Guillaume is on the mend and that his shoulder wound shows no sign of infection. If he takes care to listen to his mother, he should be out and about by next week."

"That's wonderful, Guillaume," Naomi agreed.

"I don't know. I'm thinking that I took a mighty tough beating. I just may have to stay in this chair, for at least a month," Guillaume winked at his father and cast a helpless look toward his mother.

"I don't mind the company, but if you choose to be sittin' there, you'll be windin' yarn and doin' the mendin'!" Eloise called her son's bluff, in a local tone.

"No, Mum. I'm feeling better already." Guillaume insisted, straightening in his chair, watching the women move into the kitchen, where they could converse privately at the table. Naomi delivered the letters from her pocket and watched the smile disappear from Eloise's face, when she read the return address on the larger of the two letters. Although naturally concerned, Naomi remained silent, honoring her friend's privacy. Eloise sighed, shoved the letters into her apron pocket, and pasted on an unconcerned smile to begin a lengthy characterization of the wondrous Dr. Kelly. Naomi then, informed her confidant about the contents of the telegram, Edward's timely return and her invigorating afternoon with the charming Master of "Broccoli Hall."

The men discussed the outcome of last year's Olympic Games in Stockholm and Guillaume's future career in architecture. Edward was impressed with Guillaume's personable nature, but not at all surprised, considering the young man's virtuous parents. On several occasions Edward and Naomi's eyes met; an instant mutual grin would steer them back to the current conversation.

The friends joined together for tea and lattit kitt (a sweet made from milk products, flavored with nutmeg). After light-hearted, whimsical, yet creative plans to capture Guillaume' assailants, the guests bid the Zigmann family "goodnight," and then left the cottage, pausing to speak in the garden.

"Guillaume has become a fine specimen, don't you think, Edward?" Naomi dropped her head with an obscure shake, thinking that "specimen" was a poor word choice. Strangely, she found herself becoming increasingly nervous with Edward; her newfound feelings were undeniably contributing to her discomfort.

"Quite the gentleman." She added trying to recover from her first attempt to initiate the dialogue.

"I agree. I hope he plans to make this his home, for a while. Eloise and Albert deserve such a treat." *Treat?* Edward too, was having difficulty with the conversation. Their new interest was obviously creating unseen barriers between them.

Edward closed the iron gate behind them, and reached for Naomi's hand, which he held to his lips and kissed softly, wishing that he could pull her close and kiss her with the passion of a loving husband.

"Thank you for today, Naomi. I haven't had so much fun, since I was a lad of twelve."

"Oh, what happened when you were a young man of twelve?" she coaxed.

"Another time, I have to retain some mystery about me!"

"Some mystery? Why mystery is your middle name!" Naomi grinned.

"Actually it's Caleb."

"That's nice... Edward Caleb. I like that. I never thought to ask what the "C" represented." Edward raised his eyebrows, surprised with her approval.

"Now, Naomi Beatrice... sleep well, sweet one, I'll see you tomorrow."

Naomi was pleased that he had remembered hers, and then regretfully felt her hand slip from his, as he parted. He stopped briefly on his walk home to turn and wave. Naomi watched Edward disappear into the woods when suddenly; he burst out of the darkness, like a grouse from the bulrushes, rushing toward her with seemingly frantic urgency. The winded messenger skidded to a stop at her feet, caught his breath, and stood tall, straightening his coat.

"Would you please give me the pleasure," pausing for another deep breath, "of dining with me for breakfast? Uh... at my home," Then adding faintly, seeking her consent, "I'm cooking."

"Well... we won't be having stew, will we?" she teased.

"My Lady, you cut me to the quick! Please give me a little credit for creativity. It may be a side dish, but certainly not the entrée," he boasted indignantly, and then broke into a mischievous smile, staring into her laughing, green eyes.

"In that case, what time do you desire my presence, sir?" she implored.

"All of the time," he answered with serious sincerity. Naomi smiled modestly.

Edward supplied a more specific hour, "Would six-thirty be too early?"

"Six thirty! Well, I guess, considering the charismatic host, I won't mind getting up with the roosters!"

"Capital!" Edward cheered. Like an inexperienced schoolboy, he grabbed her and hugged her. Releasing her, he hurried off into the woods, to return home to prepare for the meal.

Naomi was overwhelmed with youthful feelings of first love, a thrill that she had not experienced, since her relationship with Hiram, when she was sixteen. She sat at her dressing table, about to blow out the lamp, when she took a second look at the contented woman in the mirror. She smiled at her reflection as she brushed her thick hair.

God had given her a new lease on life. Before noon, she was questioning His motives, but now it was apparent that Edward McDonnally had an important role in her future happiness.

I think he loves me, and he already loves Allison, Naomi smiled, as she took a fountain pen and writing paper from the drawer in front of her. Without further delay, she began her letter:

> *Dearest Allison,*
>   *I too, have the most wonderful news! I think that I am in love! Edward is*

She stopped abruptly and slowly ran a line through Edward's name, then another.

I can't tell her. No one can know that he's alive, yet. Disheartened, she tore the stationery into small pieces and dropped them into the dustbin with the disappointment of withholding her feelings from her only child. She took the tiny stamp from her pocket, placed it on the dressing table and wandered over to the window, viewing the full moon and the late September sky, twinkling gloriously with constellations. Yes, her world was full of beauty and hope.

Maybe, next week, when Allison arrives, I will introduce Edward to her and her new beau. But whom shall he be? Edward Caleb McDonnally or Lucas McClurry? She blew out the flame and climbed onto the feather mattress, pulling her knees up to her chest. Patience played skillfully with a loosened thread from the comforter at the foot, in the moonlight pouring across the bed.

"Patience, I think that we have entered a new path, one leading us away from this room and McDonnally Manor." Naomi slipped under the covers and closed her eyes to give thanks, when she sat up with a startled reflex. She stared at the bed before her, with a disquieting realization; she was sleeping in his bed, Edward's bed! It had never occurred to her before. Her feelings husband or not, induced a sense of shame and impious guilt. Without hesitation, she jumped from the bed, dragging the pillow and comforter with her, dashing for the door to the hall. She stopped in her tracks, glared down at the linens, let out a short gasp and turned to throw them back on the bed. She snatched her shawl from the chair, as her bare feet delivered her to the safety of the guest room at the top of the stairs. Patience enjoyed the lively game, following close on Naomi's heels, bounding through the corridor.

Naomi pulled back the blanket and top sheet and settled into her new sleeping quarters with a sigh of relief.

Come, Payshee, let's pray, we have a lot to be thankful for.

Chapter IX

"Duncan Ridge"

"And on that cheek and o'er
that brow
So soft, so calm, yet eloquent,
The smiles that win, the tints
that glow
But tell of days in goodness
spent,
A mind at peace with all below,
A heart whose love is innocent."

— Lord Byron

Naomi, with feelings characteristic to those of a young girl excited to meet the new boy in class, was up and dressed by dawn. She checked her pendant watch. *I have forty-five minutes to spare?!*

She chose a handful of carrots from the pantry and stopped to speak with Mr. Zigmann and Guillaume in the garden, who were trimming the wisteria. After a brief conversation, she delivered the vegetable treats to Edward's horses, which were grazing in the early morning sun. Naomi meticulously wiped her hands on her handkerchief to avoid soiling her beautiful pale yellow dress, and proceeded curiously toward the barn.

She peeked in, admiring the beautiful saddles and the assorted tack hanging neatly around the walls, north of the stalls. The aroma of leather and freshly cut hay filled the air. A tiny, pathetic mewing, from behind the stacked bales, caught her attention. She distinctly remembered Edward speaking of the new litter, which arrived in the hay loft, only three and a half weeks earlier, which he moved to their new residency, the straw-lined box in the tool shed.

Questions of the kitten's separation from its family ran through Naomi's mind, while she listened for the faint, yet relentless, voice that echoed in the wall behind the hay. She began a methodical search for the tiny creature, which seemed to be calling to her in dire need. Gathering her skirts, she climbed up on the stacked bales watching and listening, guided to the far left corner of the pile. After heaving bale after bale by the twine straps to the floor, Naomi's frustration increased, each time the helpless baby moved closer, and then disappeared into the depths again.

She tugged with four more bales; one by one, she slid them down from the pile, straining under the weight, desperate to rescue the lost, possibly trapped kitten. Upon lowering the fourth bale, she noticed a wooden shaft behind the stack. The tiny victim, calling for help, was apparently inside of it, out of Naomi's reach. Climbing high upon the bales, struggling, she made one final attempt, to get visual confirmation of the possessor of the wailing voice. Recognizing that her efforts were in vain, she sat back, totally exhausted.

The little voice continued to plea, while Naomi prayed for assistance. Within a minute, Edward appeared at the barn door, dumbfounded to see his distraught breakfast guest, covered in dust and stems of hay from head to toe. She appeared to be wearing that which one might describe as a primitive striped bee costume. Without thought to her earthy appearance, Naomi welcomed the sight of her host.

"Thank God, you're here," she breathed with relief.

"I will, when I understand the difficulty." Edward studied the situation, oblivious to the source of her dilemma.

"It's the kitten. I can't find it and it needs its mother."

"What kitten?"

"Listen. It's trapped behind the bales."

They listened intently for the alleged cat, until the mewing filled the corners of the barn. Edward went to the corridor, between the old cow troughs and the grain crib and opened a small, inconspicuous door that leaned against the stack. Out crept a tiny white ball of fluff, with butter-scotch ears and scattered other fawn markings. Edward, speaking comforting words, picked it up carefully with his large hands, carried the mewing infant over to Naomi, and placed it in her lap. Her dirty face brightened with the success, while she examined the tiny, clear blue eyes of the lost soul.

Edward ushered his dusty guest to the tool shed to deliver the precious cargo. Once there, Naomi lowered the small kitten next to its mother, for some much-needed nourishment. Mama cat licked her misplaced offspring, then looked to Naomi, as if to say "thank you." Watching the joyful reunion, Edward hugged his disheveled companion, the tender-hearted Naomi, holding back tears of gladness and relief.

The contrasting couple left the little family and walked up to Edward's home. Naomi's appear-ance went unnoticed, until she caught sight of her shadow moving slowly before her, revealing the head of a scarecrow rather than a prim and proper British woman. Naomi offered a spiel of apologies, all of which Edward graciously accepted, but deemed unnecessary. He denied her request to re-turn to McDonnally Manor for a change of clothes, insisting that clean hands and face were all that he required, along with a good brushing off with the broom, which he gladly provided.

"We're quite a pair aren't we? If it's not soot it's dust!" Edward chortled.

After a quick clean-up, they entered the din-ing room and sat down to say grace at the long oak dining table, neatly set with sparkling china and a spread of fine food.

Noticing a large green cloth bound book, to the right of her place setting, Naomi inquired, "What's this?" aware of it's obvious placement.

"Oh, that, that's nothing," Edward tempted her, removing the volume with deliberate leisure and returning it to an opening between two novels on the upper bookshelf. Naomi allowed him to place it on the shelf and return to the table, before responding to his transparent motives. Edward took his place across from her, trying to hide his shame in the strategic placement of the book and gave a prayer of thanks for the breakfast and the special company.

When they raised their heads, Naomi showed unexpected interest, "Edward, the mysterious book that you returned to the shelf, intrigues me. What is it?" Naomi inquired with sweet sincerity.

"It's just my stamp collection," he added, dampening the drama of the "mystery" wondering if his guest would find it of interest.

"You are a philatelist! How delightful! How long have you pursued this endeavor?" Naomi inquired, between bites.

Edward straightened in his chair with enthusiasm. "Most of my life; I've always found it to be a relaxing, entertaining pastime. Would you care to take a look when we've finished breakfast?"

Naomi swallowed, blotted her mouth with the linen napkin, and agreed wholeheartedly, "Why, most certainly, Edward."

"Capital!" Edward's soft smile broadened to an ear-to-ear smile, pronouncing the deep dimple in each cheek, peeking beyond his red beard. Discovering Naomi's genuine interest, Edward proudly admitted that he had been an avid collector since a small child and the majority of his stamps had been purchased or donated from the tourists, met in his travels.

"I've shied away from any major purchases for rare stamps. Mine's a rather modest collection," he apologized. Naomi smiled compassionately.

She joined Edward for woodcock (anchovies, covered with scrambled eggs on toast) and fresh fruit compote, drenched in cream. They retired to the parlor for tea and almond cake, Edward's specialty, then to examine the album. An hour passed without notice, as they poured over the tiny masterpieces from all corners of the world, pointing out favorites and identifying architecture and past rulers.

When Edward closed the album, Naomi insisted, "Thank you for the beautiful breakfast and for sharing your collection with me." Feeling embarrassed about her appearance, "Edward, now I need to go and change into something more presentable." She patted his hand, and rose to leave, as graciously as possible, in spite of her attire.

"The pleasure was all mine. I have never shown my collection to anyone; I'm glad that you were the first to see it. Now, I'll escort you home and maybe you could exchange that *lovely* dress for a riding habit and well... if you'd like we could take a ride up to Duncan Ridge?" his confidence slightly wavering.

"I would love to. I've been dreaming about touring the moors on one of your horses," Naomi heartily agreed.

As they continued across the cobblestones, Naomi asked curiously, "What compelled you to look for me in the barn, this morning?

He explained that after she was nearly a half hour late for their engagement, he had searched the woods, out of concern for her safety, and then had spoken with the Zigmanns, who of course had reported her presence at the barn. In reality, her safety was not the primary issue, knowing the woods were benign, but more his fear of being stood up, even after such a short delay.

Upon reaching the manor portal, Edward dropped Naomi's hand, turned to her, and framed her blushing face with his strong hands, tenderly kissing her forehead, with closed eyes; for Edward, it was a kiss to remain there for eternity. He slowly freed her and encouraged her to make haste, for he would be returning with the horses at eleven.

Naomi ran upstairs with his departure and pulled the riding apparel from her trunk. She paused to set her boots on the floor and lifted out Allison's folded baby blanket, her daughter's only possession, when Naomi adopted her. The orphanage had reported that Allison, as an infant, was found outside of a tent belonging to the Barnum and Bailey Circus, which had been playing in London. A young man had delivered her to the authorities, wrapped in the hand woven blanket with the surname O'Connor embroidered on it. After an eight-week investigation, no evidence of her parents was found.

Naomi set the blanket aside, to remove a large indigo velvet pouch, which lay beneath it. Naomi carried it to the settee, pulled the tooled, leather bound album from its bag, opened it slowly and scanned the first few pages with a newfound appreciation. Remembering that time was of the essence, she closed it quickly and placed it back in the luxurious sack and pulled the golden tassels of the drawstrings. Naomi returned it to the trunk and began disrobing expeditiously.

Someday I'll give it to him...a special gift for all that he's done for Allison and me.

The velvet pouch held an extraordinary album, a gift to Naomi's mother, Beatrice, in honor of her ten years of excellent service to the Landseer household. Mrs. Landseer had taken note of the maid's interest in the stamps on the correspondence of her daily deliveries and had mounted the stamps in the album, without Beatrice's knowledge; Naomi's mother was overwhelmed with gratitude for the loving gesture and valuable collection.

When Beatrice disappeared, it was Mrs. Landseer who financed the fruitless search. She never fully recovered from the emotional loss of her loyal companion. Through the years, she had found some consolation in a frequent exchange of letters with Beatrice's daughter, Naomi, and had adorned the envelopes with special stamps in honor of her treasured friend. However, the forlorn mistress would open each of Naomi's letters with hopeful anticipation that there would be news of Beatrice's return, of which there was none. Several years later, the Landseers left the British Isles to travel to America, where they found a pleasant cottage, near Boston to call their new home.

Naomi was ready and waiting in the drive when Edward arrived on his prize Hanoverian, leading the handsome, bay Percheron. Naomi used the entry step to mount the large horse, and then trotted off jovially to Duncan Ridge, on that very special, first ride with Edward.

The landscape seemed to be at it's optimum beauty in the eyes of the appreciative couple; reaching their destination by way of nearly five miles of breathtaking countryside. When they arrived at the top of the ridge, they spent several minutes gazing over the moors below.

After Edward helped Naomi dismount, they walked to a small meadow of heather and tied their horses to a nearby tree. They sat down, side by side, on a large boulder to admire the uninhabited hillside, dotted with a rainbow of wild flowers, waving in the brisk October winds.

"It is so beautiful, Edward," Naomi remarked, removing her hat and placing it by her side.

'You're so beautiful, Naomi." Naomi dropped her head, unprepared for his comment.

"I mean it, Naomi. You are the most beautiful woman, that I have ever known," he reiterated with a matter-of-fact tone, reaching for her hand. Naomi raised her eyebrows with a hint of disbelief, but found his fierce convictions satiating, with her hand melting in his.

"I don't know what to say..."

"Say that I'm the most beautiful man that you have ever known! And we'll call it even!" he laughed uneasily.

"Oh, Edward, you never cease to amaze me, with your silliness!"

"Alright, so say I'm the silliest man that you've ever known, but... say that you love me." Naomi sat silent with a series of fleeting thoughts.

He's the Voice. The red-bearded Lucas McClurry...my late husband Edward. Hiram's uncle... my benefactor. And I do love him... But, I can't say the words...I can't, not yet.

Edward realized at that moment, that he had overstepped his bounds by Naomi's perplexed look.

I have gone too far, too soon. She wasn't ready to hear it. Maybe she will never be. Maybe I am deluding myself; maybe she loves me, but only as a brother.

Before Edward became totally consumed in regret, Naomi pointed to a small gathering of ducks, running through the meadow below. "Look, over there, are those the new Khaki Campbells coming this way?"

Squinting at the frolicking fowl, Edward, relaxed by the change of subject, "Yes, I think so, Mr. Kilvert bought a half dozen last spring; their eggs are supposedly superb. They probably heard through the grapevine to follow us, in hopes of joining us for another picnic," he suggested sarcastically.

"They probably have come to request a juggling encore, by Edward the Magnificent!" Naomi rejoined.

"More than likely they received news from the farm animals that Naomi McDonnally would be providing a fashion show with the latest "earthy styles," he shot back smiling.

"Maybe so, but they probably came strictly for the refreshments. You know, the master of Broccoli Hall's world famous stew," Naomi giggled, "And speaking of amusing apparel... skinny Albert."

"Touché!" Edward surrendered willingly in the battle of wits.

The laughter and teasing about their past misadventures floated silently away with the large cumulous overhead. She inquisitively studied the tiny laugh lines, beaming like rays from the sun, around his eyes. She felt that the deep creases, that marked his obvious maturity, were unjustly and unnaturally characteristic for someone with such enterprising youthful energy and childlike nature, apparent earlier, when inviting her to breakfast and sharing his prized collection. Edward's arm slid stealthily around her shoulders. Now, sitting quietly in the confines of the crux of his protective arm, she basked in the security and peace of this cherished time with the undeniably, yet pleasantly older "gentle, man." The physical, emotional and mental proximity they shared fell gently around them like a warm woolen shawl, tightening the bond that brought them to the moment, which both parties prayed to be eminent. Naomi snuggled closer under Edward's strong embrace.

Naomi's shy, but confident smile widened, as her green eyes twinkled, peeking up, beneath the fluttering plaid neck scarf, at her newfound love. Her heart raced, as their eyes met when he leaned down, slipped his hand around her neck, and pulled her slowly towards him.

Their kindred spirits became one, as Edward and Naomi closed their eyes to seal their mutual commitment to their future together, with a long awaited kiss, while the autumn breezes passed gently over them.

"I love you, Edward," the words flowed smoothly through her lips, speaking ever so softly. Edward turned away to wipe the uncontrolled tears, now streaming down his cheeks; appearing suddenly with the blessing of her acceptance. He enclosed his trembling arms around her and stroked her hair, as her head lay pressed against his chest.

"I love you too... Mrs. McDonnally," he whispered.

Naomi and Edward ended their visit to Duncan Ridge with a silent ride home, exchanging amorous glances, unaware of the world around them.

Chapter X

"The Secret"

"As fair art thou, my bonnie lass,
So deep in luve am I;
And I will luve thee still, my dear,
Till a' the seas gang dry:

Till a' the seas gang dry, my dear,
And the rocks melt wi' the sun;
I will luve thee still, my dear,
While the sands o' life shall run."

— Robert Burns

The following morning, Eloise moved the rest of Naomi's personal affects to the guest room. She prepared the unoccupied master bedroom for Allison's beau, and the room, adjoining Naomi's, for Allison.

During an afternoon inspection of the guest rooms, Naomi, with her kitty companion, took a detour up to the third floor for another look at the beautiful ballroom. There she spun around the floor, dancing with her imaginary partner, none other than the Master of Brachney Hall.

On her return to the staircase, Naomi eyed a key attached to an emerald green tassel, sticking in the keyhole of the second door on the right. She discarded any notion of entering the room, when her curiosity of the intrigue behind the locked door, got the best of her. Convincing her that the obvious accessibility gave justification for entry, Naomi, cautiously, turned the silver key. Its uninviting coolness between her fingers seemed to be dissuading her from venturing further; however, after checking the hall in both directions for suspecting eyes, she unlocked the door, in the manner of an unsure trespasser. The silk tassel clung to her palm, dampened with nervous perspiration.

Opening the dark oak door with her left hand and wiping her right hand on her skirt, she peered in, and then entered, noticing the distinct scent of rosewater. Surprisingly, the room in question, lit by the midmorning light, was dusted and in order.

Eloise must make this part of her weekly housekeeping routine, she thought, making note of the feminine décor, classic in style, enhanced by the floral fragrance. The ivory linen drapes, that matched the ornately quilted coverlet and canopy of the bed, seemed untouched by time.

Patience leaped onto the beautiful spread, then, spotting an insect on the carpet, shot under the bed to retrieve it. Naomi continued to survey the area, noting the small, Duncan Phyfe writing desk, the portrait of Hiram's mother above it, and a beautiful gold leaf hand mirror on the dressing table.

This was his mother's room? Why was her bedroom on the third floor, while the master bedroom was on the second? These questions, of such personal nature, seeded the onset of unsurpassable regret of the unwelcome intruder.

After several attempts to coax Patience to follow her to the door, Naomi crawled under the bed in search of her feline friend, which continued to ignore her whispers. With an outstretched arm to recover her pet, her fingers fell on something cold which gave cause for her immediate retraction. After quickly withdrawing her hand, she peered under the lifted edge of the coverlet, to spy a brass case, located midway beneath the bed, blocking her view of the belligerent cat. She sat up, scanned the room, and then slid back under the bed. Her defiant fingers ran across the case, once again, and unscrupulously, brought the mysterious object into view.

Naomi sat up with the forbidden article cradled comfortably in her lap. She supported her position leaning back on her hands, planted firmly on the floor, refusing to touch the tempting treasure; however, having no qualms about a thorough visual inspection. She examined the case, which resembled a small humpback trunk, complete with leather handles attached to the sides. The absence of lock and key brought raised brows and a slight biting of her lower lip. Naomi's green eyes moved vigilantly around the room, once again, as she scooted to a balanced sitting position and gently lifted the box from her lap. As she turned over the mystifying chest for further scrutiny, Patience flew out from beneath the bed skirt, in hot pursuit of its prey, leaped wildly at her, knocking the case from Naomi's hands to the floor. The unexpected impact left the case upside down on the carpet, with its contents scattered around it.

Naomi set about, nervously, returning a pink ribbon and a tiny pair of booties to the case, when her eyes fell upon a crumpled page beneath the box. Its wrinkled appearance was obviously not a result from the skirmish, but the product of a very distressed hand of the past. Without another thought, she violated all acts of privacy and slowly opened and smoothed the paper to reveal the unbearable secret.

My darling Amanda,

It is very late, my dear, and I have regretfully exhausted every avenue of the search. I have visited every village and town from the Channel, to the northern mountains of the island and have not met a single soul, who has seen anyone, matching the description of our sweet baby Hannah with that so-called wretched 'nanny' Vila. I so wish that I had more promising news; but I fear that Vila has left the mainland and that she is hiding in Europe. The contacts, which I have made in France and Germany, have nothing to report and consider our search of many months to now be futile.

Please be comforted, during this unbearable time, with the love and prayers that I send to you with this letter and give a hug and kiss to our little Hiram. My orders are sending my dear friend, Hiram and I, immediately to South Africa. I know that my absence is aggravating the situation and adding further distress for little Hiram, already sensing the loss of his twin sister. But rest assured, that I shall return to you as soon as possible. Together, we will find the strength to love, enjoy and protect our baby boy and forever cherish the memory of our little Hannah. I pray with you, that her despicable abductor is taking good care of her.

Your Loving
Husband,

Geoffrey

Naomi's hands trembled as she reread the disconcerting letter.

Poor Amanda, her baby kidnapped! Who is Vila? Why would she take her? She questioned the framed image of Hiram's mother; her maternal instincts aroused.

Naomi carefully folded the wrinkled paper reverently and placed it in the case with the other items. The news of the kidnapping of Hiram's twin weighed heavily on her heart, bringing back memories of her mother's disappearance.

The unspoken truth of Amanda's despondency which led to Hiram's childhood years in London with his grandmother was now apparent. In spite of the many questions that arose with this information, Naomi, guilty of invasion of privacy, remained silent in regard to the delicate subject. She left the room, asking for God's forgiveness for her indiscretion and returned to the main floor, cuddling Patience in her arms.

Months had gone by without any word from Hiram. The consensus was that his returning before the year was out was only a remote possibility. Mr. Zigmann paused from his duties of filling the oil lamps in the front hall to explain that unfortunately, for Naomi, his uncle had taken leave, as well.

"Mrs. McDonnally, your husband has left Brachney Hall temporarily. He sends his apologies, but promises to meet with you soon." Naomi felt her heart breaking as the caretaker continued. For the first time, she truly felt that she had a husband and now, he was gone.

"The village gossip suggests that Nathan MacKenzie has taken an uncommon interest in Brachney Hall and that he is making inquiries as to its owner, in hopes of purchasing the property. Although he's planning to sell it, he prefers to keep it out of the hands of your father." The caretaker explained that Edward, heeding this warning, would remain temporarily incognito. Although saddened by his absence, Naomi understood and supported his decision to honor his vow to avoid conflict, or physical confrontation, if at all possible. She held her tongue, regarding her father's part in Edward's absence with hopes of channeling her energy to constructive means, rather than sheer vengeful anger.

During Edward's retreat, Naomi was pleased to discover that the young Guillaume shared a mutual love of poetry. They enjoyed many an afternoon taking turns, reciting a variety of verses; from Emily Dickens' short piece, *Chartless* to the many stanzas of Thomas Moore and Robert Burns. The first Sunday in October, Naomi and Guillaume were spending a typical, fireside afternoon together, when Guillaume recited Moore's, *The Light of Other Days*, a poem depicting the maudlin memories of a man's boyhood. A morose feeling fell over Naomi, listening to the sensitive orator read what seemed to be an uncanny depiction of Hiram's life. Strangely, Guillaume obviously shared a personal interest in the poem as well, reading it with more expression than usual. On completion of the final stanza, they sat lost in silence. Neither party questioned the other as to the origin of their deep thoughts, but the sense of a strong emotional connection with the poem, was quite apparent.

Each afternoon reading ended with conversations over tea, frequently diverging from the poetry, to discussing Naomi's pride and joy, Allison. Naomi willfully divulged the many virtues and idiosyncrasies of her daughter to the young Zigmann, increasing his interest in Allison's arrival, with each anecdote. Naomi's anticipation to meet Allison's beau had peaked too. Guillaume, on the other hand, found Jack Rands upcoming visit to be anything but thrilling and although his thoughts of future moments with Allison were aggravated by the existence of "Mr. Wonderful," he maintained a positive attitude, in the prospect of developing a relationship with the fascinating Miss O'Connor.

Chapter XI

"Heidi"

"Give love, and love to your life
will flow,
A strength in your utmost need;
Have faith, and a score of hearts
will show
Their faith in your work
and deed."

— Madeline Bridges

Late, one afternoon in early October, Naomi and Guillaume were in the study, discussing his prospects of employment with an architectural firm in America, when Patience passed through the hall, carrying what appeared to be unfortunate prey that apparently, had fallen victim to one of her games. Naomi's pet ritualistically, brought "gifts" from the meadow, nearly every week, for her beloved owner; today was obviously no exception.

With this observation, Naomi slid her elbows up on the table, rested her head in her hands, and sighed hopelessly, wondering if the catch was a poor bird or rodent. Guillaume smiled and offered to dispose of the present, as he did so many times before, then patted Naomi on the shoulder with an encouraging, "Not to worry," and left the study in pursuit.

After several minutes, Naomi became curious, when her young friend had not returned with a report. She ventured out into the hall, where she saw Guillaume coming from the kitchen.

"By George, I have lost the rascally cat," he gestured apologetically.

"She's probably upstairs," Naomi determined, leading the way up the staircase to her guest room. There they found Patience, with her back to the door, sitting on the bed.

"Wait here, please, I'll see what the specialty of the day is," Guillaume recommended. The young Zigmann proceeded to the bed, and paused, astounded, when the suspected prey came into view.

"Good grief!" Guillaume remarked, as he folded his arms over his chest, looming over the cat and her find.

"What is it?" Naomi inquired hesitantly, upon reviewing his reaction.

"Come see for yourself, Madame," he suggested, smiling coyly at the concerned pet owner. Naomi approached the bed, unknowingly. She too, was taken by surprise to find her pet, grooming a tiny appreciative pup, a black and tan dachshund to be exact.

"Oh, dear! Patience, Mrs. Dugan is going to be furious with you! If she is not, all ready!" Naomi reprimanded. Guillaume grinned, when the tiny puppy rolled over on its back to have its belly washed. Naomi, instinctively, put her hand to her mouth to hide the forbidden smile, observing her pet's attentive behavior to the little hostage, not much larger than the surrogate mother's head.

"I have to return this wee lassie to her mother immediately, before she's missed. However, it's quite possible; its mother has worried herself into a frenzy, as we speak." Naomi lifted the wriggling fur ball from the coverlet.

"Patience, I understand your weakness for this little one, but she needs more than a nanny, she is not weaned yet," Naomi explained, her words falling on the deaf ears of the unimpressed feline. "This prized puppy is worth a fortune. Harriet Dugan is probably engaged in a frantic search; I need to return it immediately." she addressed Guillaume, heading toward the stairs.

"I'll accompany you to the Dugan's and verify your innocence in the matter," he laughed.

"Thank you, but I'm sure that she will be not at all surprised to find that Patience is the culprit!" she glared down at her cat, which followed close on her heels, displeased with the confiscation of its new baby. Guillaume held the puppy, while Naomi slipped into her olive, woolen jacket and tied a white silk scarf around her head. Guillaume returned the precious pup to Naomi, now wrapped securely in his muffler, opened the door for the bundled pair and buttoned his overcoat. They began their mission to the Dugan home, leaving Patience to tour the mansion, in search of another distraction.

"Did you know that the Dugan home was, at one time, the McDonnally guest cottage?" Naomi asked Guillaume, walking briskly on her right, head down with his cap tipped over his brows, to shelter his face from the seasonable chill.

"Yes, mother had mentioned some connection with Margaret, the maid for the McDonnallys?" Guillaume asked, tucking his hands in the pockets of his overcoat.

"Geoffrey, Hiram's father, had offered the guest house to Margaret's aged mother to live in, so that she would be in close proximity to her daughter. Margaret and her husband, Walter, were residing in the manor house at the time. The gardener took quarters in the cottage that your parents live in. Geoffrey, eventually, willed the guest house and a small parcel of land to Margaret, who in turn, sold it to the Dugans, when she and Walter retired in Ireland."

"Are you familiar with Mrs. Dugan's extraordinary miniature collection?" Guillaume inquired, curiously.

"I've heard tell of it, but never actually had the pleasure of seeing the 'Twiglets'. Your mother explained to me that, Joseph, Mr. Dugan, a retired sailor, had been one of Harriet's customers. She was a seamstress at the time." Naomi readjusted the pup, which was wiggling out of the scarf. "She tailored a number of Mr. Dugan's jackets and did most of his mending, when he was on shore leave...settle down wee one...With each payment, Mr. Dugan had presented Harriet with a carved wooden token, either in the form of an animal or human character. She has them displayed throughout their house," Naomi added, tucking the end of the scarf, beneath the little dachshund.

They arrived at the small stone house, a five-minute walk from the manor or a stone's throw away, according to the Dugans. They stepped up to the door, beneath two, elaborately carved shingles, with the now snoozing pooch. The larger shingle bore the Dugan name in italicized letters within a wreath of blue fleur de lis; the smaller, whipping in the winds from its golden chains, denoted "The Twiglets."

"Weel, there she be," Harriet Dugan warmly greeted the visitors, opening the bright red door, before they had a chance to knock. She accepted the missing hound from beneath Guillaume's scarf with a broad, relieved smile. The appreciative woman invited Naomi and Guillaume to the kitchen to see the mother and the rest of the litter, resting comfortably in a wicker basket by the stove. She took the visitors' wraps and hung them on the coat rack, then led the way.

"I am very sorry about this, Mrs. Dugan. Patience meant no harm to the puppy. She just has a bad habit of bringing home her finds to me. She had carried it up to my bedroom and was bathing it when we found her," Naomi explained.

"Don't ye be frettin' o'r it. The pup's fine," the amused breeder reassured, not surprised to find that Naomi's pet was the perpetrator, as predicted.

Naomi and Guillaume, having entered the house for the first time were amazed upon observing the parlor walls. Each wall was fitted with shelving for a series of dioramas, giving the room the appearance of a small art museum, rather than a parlor in a private residence.

"Can you believe this, Guillaume?" Naomi whispered.

"Canna say I believe it meself... 'specially on the dustin' days," Harriet, responded, overhearing her embarrassed guest. The guests greatly admired the creativity and dedication in Harriet's canvas backdrops for the dozens of wooden figurines, depicting outdoor scenes for the wildlife, barns for the livestock and even brightly decorated rooms, for the various tiny human miniatures. Each unit was part of its own small world, beckoning the viewer to step closer out of their world, into the new one beyond Mrs. Dugan's oils. Harriet encouraged the captivated visitors, to continue on to the kitchen, after modestly thanking them for their interest and comments on the extensive art display.

"Here's the rest o' the lot," Harriet pointed to the basket of squirming activity.

"Oh, they are adorable, Mrs. Dugan!" Naomi noted, kneeling down beside the puppies, snuggling with their proud mother.

"Yes, fine looking little chaps," Guillaume agreed. "But they don't seem to have the confirmation of dachshunds. What breed is the father?" Guillaume asked innocently, bending over the basket to get a better look.

"Me dear lad, the sire is the finest black and tan dachsie in all Munich," Harriet reported defensively. "It'll be takin' several months before the snout lengthens and same be wi' the body," she added sounding as professional as possible. Before Guillaume had a chance to apologize, the hostess was busy preparing three place settings with bowls and spoons at the kitchen table, under the window.

"Now ye will be joinin' me for me special recipe of cherry and plum puddin', just took it outta the oven. Watch ye tongues, it'll be verra hot."

Her visitors had satiated their appetites at tea, but mutually consented to the invitation, tantalized by the aromatic dessert. Guillaume and Naomi took their places, while Mrs. Dugan daintily scooped a serving into each bowl and began explaining her experience with the missing pup. She sat down next to Guillaume and folded her arms.

"I was just fetchin' me wrap to join me darlin' dog, Angel, when yer kitty probably crept in the back door. Ye see, I'd be keepin' it open wi' me boot-jack, so me darlin' can come and go to her likin'. Bless her heart, she be needin' a break from her brood. Ye ne'r find a more attentive mum. Why she wouldna leave the basket wi'out askin' first."

Harriet paused, unfolded her arms, and tasted a spoonful of pudding. "A bit too sweet... so me dear Angel, followed me to the tool shed, where I noticed the door would be open. That's when I'm suspectin' Paysh sneaked off wi' de wee one... Mr. Dugan makes a habit of closin' the shed door each night to keep the vermin from comin' in. If I be tellin' him once, I be tellin' him a dozen times. Now Joseph, ye shan't be wastin' yer day wi' that jabberin' Jon Wiggins down at the butcher shop when we be needin' repairs on the house. Faulty latch, ye know... Would ye be carin' for tea?" she asked, leaving her seat, to collect the cups from the cupboard.

"Yes please, if it would not be too much trouble," Naomi answered, turning to Guillaume, "And you?"

"No thank you, Mrs. Dugan. I'm just fine." The young man sat back in his chair and stretched a little, quite full from the sweet.

"Weel, me lovin' pup dinna want to stay wi' me and headed back to the house while I be checkin' me bedroom rug, airin' on the line. Sometimes ye haeta take care, ye ken. Ye shan't be throwin' caution to the wind, in airin' fine rugs."

The older woman hesitated a moment, then half giggled, half snorted realizing the play on words. Her sparkling eyes and infectious laugh set the visitors joining in, not quite sure about the source of Harriet's amusement. A moment later, she regained her composure and continued, while the entertained visitors struggled to follow her train of thought.

"Aye, Mr. Dugan wouldna be sayin' therna be an ounce of humor in me body had he heard that grand one, ay? Yer witnesses to it, ye be," she smiled proudly. "The point I be tryin' to make," she snickered "is that ye haeta be careful in yer timin'" to protect yer rugs from being bleached from the heat of the sun. That's when I noticed me darlin' runnin' toward the house and into the kitchen. Weel, I canna tell you how loud the cryin' and the howlin' 'twas." Harriet stopped to take a breath and a sip of tea. Naomi and Guillaume waited respectfully for Harriet's grand finale.

"I dropped me rug, to see what would be troublin' her when I made a count and couldna find the missin' babe...Then I saw yer smilin' faces." The storyteller sighed with relief and took another spoonful of pudding, now cold, but appreciated just the same.

"Patience has little mercy for most of God's creatures," Naomi admitted. "It was dreadful in London. She would bring home young rats. After a fortnight and four of the loathsome rodents, I had to confine her to the cottage. The pong of dead rats filling the cottage was more than I could bear... oh sorry, Mrs. Dugan, not a very pleasant topic for the tea table."

"Dinna worry. Mr. Dugan canna sit thro' a supper wi'out tellin' Wiggins' horrid butcherin' tales or those dreaded seafarin' accidents." Naomi and Guillaume exchanged cringing glances, praying that Mrs. Dugan would not share the accounts.

"Well, I thought it would be nice for Patience to run free across the moors," Naomi added quickly. "Unfortunately, the meadow is enticing and plentiful, to say the least; although, it does help keep her out of Mrs. Zigmann's hair," Naomi rationalized.

"Aye, Eloise has dozens of tales about That Cat... Fur? cat fur... aye, Jamie McFurlyn. I've been makin' pairs of words...to remind me. Aye, one of Mr. Dugan's mateys, 'twas the one who named the Twiglets," she rolled her eyes upward and scowled slightly. "Ah, yes, Jamie, God Bless him...only seventeen, he was...poor laddie, lost at sea... hard work, ye know, carvin them; the crew teasin' me poor Joseph, 'til he'd be takin' to his cabin for a bit of peace when they found out that he be carvin them for me... D'ye ever see such a wonderful collection?" Her guests shook their heads and before they had an opportunity to respond further, Harriet continued.

"Aye, the finest carvin' in all of Scotland, I'd say! A jolly good party, we gave wi' the crew on me weddin' day..." Harriet sipped her tea slowly, remembering. "We sang and danced 'til dawn." She sat back in her chair smiling with the memories, then took her handkerchief from her apron and wiped her eyes and claimed that there were more gifts than she could count. "Blessed fools," she shook her head. "Now what'd I be sayin'?" Naomi and Guillaume shrugged, with a loss for words.

Mrs. Dugan's silence left Naomi and Guillaume staring blankly at each other, when they simultaneously concurred, "That cat."

"Aye, me dear friend Eloise may claim to despise that cat, but I'll be tellin' ye now, when the time comes for you to be headin' to London, she'll be walkin the floors, bored to tears," Harriet nodded at Naomi. "That's me reasonin' for Eloise to take on one o' Angel's pups. I'm certain Master McDonnally won't be mindin'," Harriet petitioned, with an occasional glimpse toward Eloise's son.

"I'm sure Edward wouldn't mind," Naomi agreed, when a warning tap from Guillaume's shoe and the stunned look shooting across his face alerted Naomi to her error. Before she had a chance to amend her statement, Mrs. Dugan spoke up.

"Edward?" she questioned. "But..."

"I mean, Hiram... Edward has been on my mind of late, being in the mansion and all," she recovered feebly.

"Sorry Mum, about yer being widowed and all, at such a young age. Ye know, everyone believed that ye and Master Hiram would be hitchin' up. Wasna secret how much he loved ye...aye, when we lived near Grimwald," Guillaume cut off Harriet Dugan mid-stride, detecting Naomi's discomfort.

"About mother, not a bad idea... she cherished our dog, Rusty. He was a stray that mother took in, when I was only five or six years old. He was a mangy mutt, but mother nursed him back to health, too. We had him for years. It broke her heart the day that he passed on; she cried for days." The subject had successfully shifted, but Guillaume's recount left a melancholy nostalgic silence. The women looked on sympathetically at the forlorn young man; empathizing with the "family's" loss. Now, it was Harriet's turn to change the subject.

"How about you, Mum? Ye seemed to take a likin' to me little Heidi, yer cat, as well. She willna visit the fields na more, if she was keepin' company wi' a wee pup," Harriet began her sales pitch.

"Oh, I don't think so. They are precious, but, I am alone now, well, with exception to my naughty cat," Naomi confirmed, beginning to teeter in her decision, with closer examination of the frolicking basket. Guillaume smiled inquisitively, watching the sale progress.

In a rather pathetic attempt to lure Harriet from her strident merchandising, Naomi lifted the older volume of John Campbell's *Popular Tales of the West Highland*, from its position, leaning against the windowsill. "What's this? A favorite of yours?"

Harriet studied her customers face and bluntly answered, "Aye," then continued to tempt her, " Would ye care to hold her again?" she offered with an impish grin.

Naomi replaced the book, "You said her name is Heidi?" Naomi mentally singled out the pup from the litter, imagining calling after the little dog.

"Let me fetch the sweet babe. Angel may be a bit leery after the separation." Harriet cupped the wriggling dachshund in her hands and placed it in Naomi's, well aware that her resistance was descending. "She'd be a wonderful companion for ye, Mum? Ye know Patience is gettin' on in years and would be enjoyin' a bit of entertainment in her retirement," Harriet added diplomatically.

Naomi held Heidi up to her face, one hand gently around its torso, the other supporting its hindquarters. She stared into the sparkling brown eyes in search of the right answer, while Heidi looked nervously away from the attentive human. Naomi cuddled the puppy close to her chest. It was quite apparent that Harriet Dugan was an expert at reading people. Mr. Dugan had claimed that his wife had missed her calling; her true lot in life was to be a door-to-door peddler.

"I hear ye'd be spendin' a lot of time with that good-lookin', Lucas McClurry of Brachney Hall. Ye know, Mum, there is nigh on nothin' as romantic as strollin' in the moonlight wi' a gentleman. Wi' an exceptional little beauty like Heidi, there'd be many a call for a long walk," Harriet concluded, planting seeds for the future.

"Mrs. Dugan! You are too creative for your own good!" Naomi chuckled, seriously agreed that purchasing the puppy may not be only an advantage to the seller. The puppy's whimper dropped Naomi's resistance to a non-recoverable low.

"All right, Mrs. Dugan, you win. Sold, one little Heidi." Naomi surrendered; an outcome Guillaume expected and music to Harriet's ears. The victorious merchant smacked her skirt-clad leg, throwing her head back with a burst of laughter, announcing, "It doesna ever fail!"

Naomi denounced, "Harriet Dugan, you are unconscionable!" scowling between smiles, shaking her head like one who had been sold a bill of goods, but not yet suffering from buyer's remorse. Guillaume, witness to the entire process, congratulated the cunning merchant on her technique. Harriet curtseyed, graciously, thanking him for the compliment.

"Thank you, Mrs. McDonnally. It keeps a lil' jam on the table. I'll be savin' Heidi for ye for five and a half weeks 'til she be weaned. Then ye can be takin' her home. If ye dinna fetch 'er then, I'll be puttin' 'er on the market. Aye, Heidi's the weeest one. Many prefer the runt of the litter," the shrewd businesswoman warned, despite her familiarity with the McDonnally family. Naomi placed Heidi back in the basket, next to the concerned mother, when Harriet suggested that Naomi bring, Patience for frequent visits, over the next few weeks to avoid the cat's change of heart. Naomi agreed, while Guillaume helped her with her wrap.

"I'll be keepin' Angel wi' the others in the bedroom, when ye visit," she reassured Naomi. "Did ye know, Mrs. McDonnally, that cad Nathan has been snoopin' round here? Aye, he's been askin' to purchase me home...for a fair price, too. But, Mr. Dugan and I are quite content here wi' the Twiglets."

Naomi remained silent with the depressing report.

"Well, thank you, Mrs. Dugan, for a lovely afternoon. The treat was quite tasty and I thoroughly enjoyed the collection. Shall we go Naomi?" Guillaume motioned to Naomi, lost in unpleasant thoughts of her father.

"Yes...Thank you Mrs. Dugan and I guess I have Patience to thank for our visit and the newest member of my little family, as well. The sweet was delicious, maybe you could give Eloise the recipe," Naomi suggested.

"I'll scribble it on one of those fancy cards that the vicar's wife sells down at the mercantile, the ones wi' the pressed posies on 'em. Mr. Dugan gave me a box of ten for me birthday, sweet man," Harriet smiled proudly.

"That will be just perfect. Now, don't be a stranger, drop by the manor house. I would love for you to meet my daughter, Allison," Naomi encouraged. The mere mention of the girl, sent Guillaume's head swimming with new ideas to strengthen the non-existent relationship with Allison. Visions of walking around the meadow with the two little dachshunds, taking Allison to her first viewing of the Twiglets, and even preparing Mrs. Dugan's recipe together in the cottage, all seemed to be worthwhile pursuits.

Creative cooking worked for Naomi and Edward. It just may work for us, he cleverly deduced.

"Mind yer head, lad," Mrs. Dugan warned Guillaume, just before his head caught the edge of the dangling shingle. Harriet waved her handkerchief at the departing visitors, and then returned to the kitchen to jot down the recipe.

"She's quite a character, isn't she?" Guillaume commented to his female companion.

"Quite the saleslady," Naomi added, feeling a bit empty-handed without the squirming puppy. It wasn't until the mansion came into view that Guillaume thought to congratulate his friend on her recent purchase.

"So you are the proud owner of a beautiful dachsie. Congratulations. I'll bet you are ecstatic about informing Allison," Guillaume's one track mind resurfaced. "I would wager that Patience feels that we kidnapped her baby," Guillaume suggested. The knee jerk reaction to the word *kidnap* triggered thoughts of Amanda and her baby Hannah.

Naomi blurted, "What?" She stopped short, seeing the young Zigmann's startled reaction, then quickly apologized.

"Don't worry, Naomi, she'll soon forget. When that pup is twice her size and living under the same roof with her, she'll be delighted with your decision," Guillaume made an effort to jokingly console his disturbed friend. She forced a grin as they entered the mansion, still haunted by the findings on the third floor.

Naomi hurried off to console her pet and break the wonderful news, realizing of course, that the exciting development would be meaningless.

Guillaume headed to the cottage to find his mother, with plans of encouraging the adoption of one of Heidi's littermates. Maybe with his help, she too would relent to Mrs. Dugan's sales abilities, thinking that two pups at the manor would double his chances with Miss O'Connor.

During the next few weeks, Patience followed Naomi to the Dugan's to visit her new playmate.

However, in the interim, the Dugans gave several reports of the impatient cat making numerous, unscheduled visits to their cottage.

Chapter XII

"The Visit"

"O clear-eyed Faith,
and Patience thou
So calm and strong!
Lend strength to weakness,
teach us how
The sleepless eyes of God
look through
This night of wrong!"

—John Greenleaf Whittier

October fourteenth arrived with a chilly dawn. By seven a.m., Naomi was restlessly anticipating her daughter's visit. Mr. Zigmann pulled the last of the weeds from the cobblestone drive, while his wife created a number of dishes and delicacies to serve the guests. During breakfast, Eloise handed Naomi a well-received note from Edward, alerting her to his promised arrival that afternoon. Having missed his companionship, Naomi was thrilled to receive the news and equally excited to have her dream fulfilled; to have the two people, whom she loved the most in the world, to finally meet.

At two twenty-five, Naomi and the Zigmann family assembled in the parlor. Naomi removed Allison's most recent postcard from her burgundy, satin dress pocket and reread it silently:

Hello Mummy,

Our itinerary does not allow us to arrive any earlier than mid-afternoon, October 14th. I cannot wait to see you! You will just love Jack!

God Bless,
Your Baby Allison

P.S. Don't be shocked by my "new" look!

The flurry of activity came to a close, with the muffled moan of a motorcar, making its way up the road to the estate, with Allison O'Connor and her beau. Eloise retied her lace apron, straightened

Guillaume's tie and buttoned the top collar button
of her husband's freshly starched shirt. Naomi took
a last peek at her hair in the hall mirror, as the
grandfather clock struck 2:30. The motorcar had
barely stopped at the portal, when the elated young
lady stepped out, and ran to the door, like a child
home from school on holiday. Reaching for the
knocker, the door flung open to reveal the glowing
face of her mother. The blissful women hugged,
holding back the tears of joy, as they examined one
another's faces.

"Baby!"

"Mummy!"

Naomi held her daughter close, listening to
her child's praises, running her fingers through the
golden curls with the nostalgic aroma of lavender
filling her head. As they embraced, Allison's beau
stepped out of the vehicle, paid the driver, and
turned toward the portal, when his eyes met
Naomi's, peering over Allison's shoulder. Her
daughter's ramblings became distorted, and then
muted in Naomi's shock and confusion. Allison released her embrace; her mother's arms fell limp,
when she turned to locate her companion. With his
approach, Allison proudly announced,

"Mother, this is Jackson Rands. Jack, this is
my mother, Naomi McDonnally."

Naomi stepped closer, in utter disbelief and
disgust. A haze of thousand words rushed through
her brain, but she spoke not one. Her initial reaction to raise a hand to strike his insolent face was
deferred by the self-control, more fitting to a reli-
gious, British woman of her breeding. She gathered
up her skirt, threw her head back defiantly and

marched into the mansion, snatching hold of Allison's hand en route.

"Mother!" Allison retaliated as Naomi led her child through the portal, slamming the door behind them and bolting it, sending the Zigmann family into a paralyzed state of shock and awe.

"Allison, please sit down! We need to discuss this situation!" her irate mother demanded, pointing to the rocker.

"Mummy, What is wrong?! How could you be so unbelievably rude?! I need to let him in!" Allison pleaded, heading toward the door.

"Absolutely, not!" Naomi reinforced. The Zigmanns excused themselves unnoticed and left promptly for the kitchen.

"Mother!" Allison turned in rebuttal glaring at her enraged mother.

"Allison, we can discuss this like two adult women... well, because we are two adult women. Never mind, the point is that Jack is not Jack!" Naomi protested, wringing her hands.

"What are you talking about? Of course, he's Jack! You don't even know him!" the irritated daughter screeched.

"I most certainly do!" Naomi insisted.

"What?" Allison's tone lowered in surprise by the implications of her mother's statement.

"He's not Jack Brands!" Naomi objected.

"That's right, he's Jack Rands!" Allison corrected sternly, confident she had resolved the confusion.

"No, no," Naomi shook her head. "He's not Jack anything, I mean anyone! He's Hiram McDonnally! He's Edward's nephew!" Naomi clarified, watching the anger envelope her daughter's now ruddy face.

"You mean that he's my cousin, by marriage...I have no problem with that, remember I'm adopted. I think that you don't either. I think that you have a problem because he's a few years older than you expected," Allison added defensively, obviously an afterthought of prior consideration.

"A few years older! Allison, he's nearly old enough to be your father and that's not—,"

Allison interrupted blurting with frustration, "I'm not listening to anymore of this rubbish!" and started to leave the parlor.

"Wait Allison, I'm your mother. Listen to me!" A moment of regret for that statement was warranted by the fear that her adopted daughter may refute it. Naomi continued before Allison could respond.

"The very reason that I came here a few months ago, was to see Hiram. We knew each other when we were much younger, over eighteen years ago. We planned to get married, but then..."

Allison faced her mother and cut in possessively, "It doesn't matter who he was eighteen years ago! He's with me now!"

"Don't be foolish, Allison, don't you see what he's doing? He's trying to punish me through you! Allison, he purposely concealed his identity by changing his name! " Naomi stormed.

"Mother, please! He didn't know that you were my mother until ten minutes ago, when I mentioned your name and read the address of our destination to the driver. He hasn't seen you in eighteen years. Do you really think that he used me as a part of some contrived malevolent scheme for revenge over an insignificant relationship between two silly children?" Allison asked with marked condescension.

The pounding of the doorknocker ended the conversation, turning their focus toward the entry hall. Eloise scurried from the kitchen, wiping her hands on her apron to unlock the door for the master of the house. She apologized for the delay, with a traditional courtesy, humbly welcomed Hiram into his own home and offered him a piece of apple-blackberry pie and tea. Hiram forgave the flustered maid, politely refused the refreshments and handed her his hat and overcoat.

"Would you please take these holdalls and put them upstai... never mind, I'll set them over here." Hiram placed the luggage on the floor next to the secretary. He nonchalantly entered the parlor, where the infuriated lioness and her cub awaited him. Eloise quickly excused herself, avoiding the anticipated fireworks, when she heard Hiram request in a suspiciously calm and collected voice, "Ladies, I need to speak with both of you, separately, please." Naomi stepped closer to her daughter, instinctively tightening the natural alliance, a bond that remained fragmented by the younger of the deceived women.

"You may speak with me, in the study," Naomi directed, trying to subdue her anger, but for the first time felt that, she had the upper hand. Allison stood motionless, not knowing what to believe at this point, watching her mother leave the room with her beau.

Eloise, a known eavesdropper, led Albert and Guillaume, from the kitchen with trays, bountiful in tea and sweets, in hopes of distracting the traumatized girl. Guillaume placed the tray on the end table and retreated to the window seat and sat, deep in thought, with clasped hands contemplating the strange course of events. He silently empathized with Allison in her state of confusion and considered his next move to initiate the relationship, with the girl who was more beautiful than he ever imagined.

"Excuse me Allison, I'm Eloise Zigmann and this is my husband, Albert, and son, Guillaume," Eloise nervously introduced her family, noting the intensity in her son's face.

The men rose to their feet, Albert nodded, Guillaume grinned, ear-to-ear, and then greeted the oblivious woman with a boisterous, "How do you do?" Allison glanced at them briefly, made a disapproving glare at the son's inappropriate cheery expression, and then barely opened her mouth to say "Hello."

She turned, fixated on the closed doors, engrossed in the possibilities of the scenes unfolding on the other side. Albert hurried over to stoke the parlor fire, while Guillaume resumed his position on the window seat, disappointed in Allison's reception of his high-spirited introduction.

"May, I help you with your jacket?" Eloise offered. Allison turned, when "jack" in "jacket" caught her attention, then nodded. Eloise helped Allison remove her outerwear, "A lovely coat, Mum. My, My it has one of those new-fangled zippers, how posh!" Eloise cautiously commented, in an attempt to distract the entranced girl, aware of Allison's pride in the new garment from her past letter. The attentive maid carried it to the hall and placed it on the hook, next to the Master's, shook her head, then

returned to pour Allison a cup of tea and guide her
to the rocking chair.

Despite Allison's inattentiveness to his presence, Guillaume was pleased to have the opportunity to simply share the same air with the lovely
daughter, who mysteriously appeared in his
dreams. Her blonde curls framed her diamond
shaped face, now slightly flushed with peach hues,
which complimented her periwinkle blouse. Guillaume looked beyond her perfect princess posture,
enhanced by the mutton-leg sleeves and the regal
ruffled collar that stood tall above the delicate
cameo brooch. With his eyes cast on the sweet,
childlike face, Guillaume reviewed the quips that
Naomi had shared with him.

His thoughts first turned to the depiction of
the little six-year old daughter, breaking loose from
Naomi's hand, to run to the fountain in the town
square. There, Allison had attempted to aid a drip-
ping lad, of twelve or thirteen, who had fallen prey
to a horde of much older bullies. Guillaume reposi-
tioned himself to get a better view of the young lady
seated in the rocker, imagining her younger coun-
terpart, longingly, offering a small hand to rescue
the boy, twice her size. Oh, how he wished that he
could have been that young boy.

She is a sweet angel, so caring, so thoughtful,
always trying to help. Is there no one way that I can
comfort her now? he painfully questioned, knowing
his limitations in the situation, yet driven to successfully extinguish her troubled frown.

Eloise sat next to her husband, working dili-
gently on the pink sweater for Maryanne Wheaton's
new baby girl, Martha, to remedy her discomfort
with the silence. The multi-colored knitting bag, sit-

ting next to her feet, sent her son back to a day, which Naomi had described so vividly, that he had felt that he had witnessed.

The incident occurred one late spring afternoon in Greenwich Park, where Allison and Naomi shared a bench. Naomi had withdrawn a luscious, red apple from her market basket and had presented it to her daughter, when the little girl turned it over several times, pondering the fruit curiously. To Naomi's surprise, Allison slid down from the bench and walked straight away to a diminutive, elderly woman, garbed in rags, napping, propped against a tree. Allison stopped a few feet from the pathetic sleeping beauty, then tiptoed closer and carefully placed the bright red piece of fruit into the tattered bag lying next to the old woman. Returning to her mother, she had remarked, "I think she's hungry, Mummy." The insight and compassion had brought tears to her mother's eyes, lifting her precious daughter to her lap and embracing her proudly, while sympathetically examining the resting peasant.

Guillaume sat, absorbed with her uncommon beauty, staring unconsciously at the enchanting young peer, disturbed by the recent injustice to a person of such unique benevolence. Suddenly, Allison cried out unexpectedly.

"Who do you think you're gawking at?" she criticized, slamming her teacup down on the saucer, sending a trail of shivers vibrating through the Zigmann clan. Guillaume, initially shocked by her outburst, rationalized that one could not expect Allison's compassionate nature to radiate during the apparent chaos.

"I'm sorry Allison," Guillaume addressed her for the first time. After that brief apology, the previous silence returned to envelope the room.

Allison, what a beautiful name. Allison, if only I could re-enact the typical "White Knight" scene and carry you to safety. His thoughts of chivalrous grandeur remained in check with the presence of the "Black Knight" in the manor, facing off with his dear friend in the study.

The tension loomed heavily over the couple in the study. In spite of Naomi's distraction with Hiram's daunting size and unexpected, refined appearance, she immediately began scorning her opponent, simmering, "How dare you?!"

"Naomi, honestly, I had no idea that Allison was your daughter. We met in a London café, a few days after I left here in August and I introduced myself as Jackson Rands, the name that I had taken to protect my privacy in Europe. I am sure that you are aware, that it has never been easy for a McDonnally to maintain a low profile."

Naomi's thoughts skirted to Edward's name change, aware that there was truth in what Hiram was saying. Hiram continued in a calming monotone, which struck Naomi, as somewhat condescending.

"Allison in turn, introduced herself, with no mention of her family. With little desire to share my family history, I never bothered to inquire about hers." A veil of disappointment fell across Naomi's face; disarmed by the fact that her daughter failed to acknowledge her existence. Her thoughts ran wild.

Is she ashamed of me or the fact that she is adopted? Oh, I hope it's not my face. She put her hand to her face, then and shook off her fears, realizing Allison *was* thrilled for Hiram to meet her.

"She never indicated that she was adopted, so I naturally assumed that the loving mother that she spoke of, was of the O'Connor clan," Hiram commented honestly with his adversary. "Your identity was not revealed, until the final leg of the journey, when I overheard the address that she had given to the driver. I know what a blow this is to you, but can you even imagine my shock, discovering that I had been enjoying the company of *your* daughter for the last couple of months and that we were heading to visit McDonnally Manor, to visit you? Why, the rest of the journey, I was torn... not knowing whether to continue, explain the situation to Allison, or have the driver return to London. The further we ventured, I realized that the there was no point in postponing the inevitable." Hiram hesitated, frustrated in defending his credibility. Naomi listened skeptically, scowling as he continued his version of the dilemma.

"You cannot possibly believe that my relationship with your daughter was created for the sole purpose of hurting you." Naomi turned defensively away from the pleading voice, remembering his anger when he left her in the debris covered parlor. "Yes, Naomi, it may very well be a cruel twist of fate, but for me, meeting your daughter was a blessing."

Naomi swung around, accusing, "Oh, I am certain that it was! Fruition for revenge!"

"Naomi, please do not jump to conclusions. You knew, by my solitary lifestyle, that I never thought that I could feel comfortable in a relationship with another woman." Naomi gasped covering her mouth with her hands, considering the unthinkable.

"But wait! You don't understand. Allison's a lovely woman; I don't have to tell you that. You have done a marvelous job raising her. Allison and I had a purely platonic relationship. There was no romance, no promises for the future. We were just good friends, enjoying each other's company. When I realized that you were her mother, I anticipated how you would react. You are justified in being upset. I had stepped beyond the natural order, not deliberately mind you, but circumstances as they were; I was enjoying the companionship of the daughter of a woman that I had loved since my youth. Albeit, a daughter with the same capacity to comfort, to share her faith and retain her high moral standards." Naomi began to soften with Hiram's acknowledgement of his love for her and the reverence and respect for her daughter's reputation.

"Naomi, please believe me, it was over the moment she spoke your name. I have not changed that much; I would never, intentionally, disrespect you or your daughter or take any action that would be detrimental to your relationship with her. Regretfully, I think it would be preferable for me to gently explain the details to Allison... and bow, gracefully out of your lives. With no disrespect to you, I think that she will be more accepting to this decision, if she knows that I'm acting on my own accord, out of concern for all of us."

Naomi's anger and resentment were diffused by the unexpected, yet tender convincing words of the "Hiram" that she once knew and loved. She stared at him, almost in disbelief, and then slowly, nodded, gratefully at her long lost friend, agreeing that it was the best solution, for a misfortunate situation.

"Naomi, about your accident, I..."

"Don't Hiram... I have lived with this face for many years and with the exception of a few fleeting insecure moments, I've learned to regard it as a humbling attribute, not a handicap or excuse."

Hiram approached her consumed with contrition, "How could I have treated you with such malice? I pray that you forgive me for my misconduct in our previous meetings and any despair that I have brought to your daughter."

With Hiram's pious plea, Naomi lowered her head, closing her eyes, equally ashamed of her ill thoughts and judgmental attitude, muttering, "Oh, Hiram..."

Hiram placed his hands on her shoulders and looked into her tearful eyes, "I truly am so very sorry, Nomee, so sorry for everything. I was blessed with the friendships of two incredibly beautiful women, two women that I will never forget."

"You owe me no apologies, Hiram... but I am worried about Allison. I think... I know that she's fallen in love with you."

"I was afraid of that, but I selfishly prolonged the relationship. Don't worry. Trust me, she's young; she'll be fine," he added with an endearing smile.

"Hiram, about Edward..."

"I understand, Naomi. I only wish that I could have thanked him." Hiram took a deep breath and left the study to meet the challenge of the younger woman's wrath. His strength and fortitude were in appearance only; he was dubious and unsure of

Allison's reaction to his resolution. Naomi followed his lead, drained by the intense pressure of all aspects of the situation. She left Edward in charge of his own dilemma, thinking, *Only one thing at a time.*

Hiram returned to the parlor with mixed expectations, not knowing if Allison believed that he had deceived her, or that she believed Naomi was at fault. Either way, he dreaded the upcoming conversation.

"Allison, will you please accompany me to the study?" he asked her with a forgiving tone.

"No. I understand that there is a garden. I would prefer to speak to you there," the tension rising with each of her statements. Hiram immediately considered her volume as a clue to the raging storm ahead.

"Yes, but it's rather chilly. I think that you would be much more comfortable in the study," Hiram half-smiled.

"Jack! Or whoever you are, I said, that I would prefer the blasted garden!" Allison slammed her teacup down on the saucer, next to the wooden box, once again. With a disdainful glare, she joined her companion of nearly three months, to the hall, where she snatched her jacket from the hook and fought to put it on quickly, avoiding Hiram's assistance. Hiram escorted the young woman of twenty-three, whose gait was uncommonly brisk and independent, to the privacy of the barren garden.

Mr. and Mrs. Zigmann exchanged disturbed glances with the equally distraught mother. Guillaume instinctively left his seat, on a mission of mercy, when his father's hand caught hold of his wrist and insisted that he remain neutral.

Upon reaching the stone bench, Hiram gestured, offering Allison a seat. They took their positions with mutual discomfort, surrounded by the October chill and emotions they had never experienced as a couple. Hiram began with a conscientious posture and responsible attitude, to cloak his wavering security.

"Allison, I have enjoyed every minute of the last three months with you, and I thank God every morning for your companionship. You have enabled me to abandon a life of solitude and revenge that I had led for years, and for that I am grateful." Allison listened without speaking, expecting the worst, ready to retaliate.

"Yes, it's true, your mother and I shared a special love in our youth and I did meet with her here in August. The meeting was nothing less than disastrous... primarily due to my insensitivity. I'm ashamed to say that I left your mother in a fit of rage and without a word as to my whereabouts. Brooding in London, I met you... you sweet wonderful girl, so attentive, so caring, so full of life and love." His voice cracked as the words came with difficulty, "You were a Godsend, like an angel to rescue me, from myself. How do you thank someone for giving you life again?" he dropped his head and hesitated. "Once again, how do you walk away from a close companion? How do you say goodbye, without appearing to be uncaring and ungrateful?"

Allison rose from the bench, melting with his charm and haunted by the inevitable, turned toward the meadow to hide the streams, trickling down her cheeks. Her eyes moved slowly from the meadow, now blanketed with a hazy mist, to the face of her first love and whispered through her tears, "You don't."

A knot formed in Hiram's stomach at the onset of Allison's trembling, and her heart breaking, from the oh-so-familiar, betrayal and deception. He lowered his eyes to the ground and shook his head slowly, rising to his feet.

"Allison, I didn't know. But now I have no choice. You understand, don't you? We have to be thankful for the memories and go our separate ways."

Allison collapsed to the bench, sobbing as Hiram walked out of her life, with the painful reality that it was best for everyone.

He returned to the main house, leaving Allison in the sanctuary of the garden without further consolation, and then motioned for assistance to Naomi, painfully watching the heart wrenching response of her daughter, from the window of the kitchen door. The older components of the obscure triangle, exchanged sympathetic glances, passing on the garden walk. Naomi sat down on the cold bench, and put her arms around her devastated daughter, with motherly hopes of pacifying the aggravation and alleviating the trauma of Allison's disappointment.

"Allison, I love you, and I only want you to be happy. Right now, you may find that difficult to believe. Sometimes, we become lost in a labyrinth of twists and turns. I know from my own experience that you must listen to your heart; you have to do what you know is right, otherwise, you will suffer the consequences and bring misery to those who share your moment in life," Naomi advised blotting her baby's tears.

"Do you love him?" Allison looked fearfully up at her mother.

"I'm not in love with him. We shared a wonderful love, many years ago, and I guess for the past eighteen years, I convinced myself that Hiram was the only man I would ever love. However, time and space came between us; our perception of the relationship became clouded with each passing year. Hiram once loved me, but that love was decimated by distrust and revenge. I realize now, that if I truly loved him, I would have disregarded my appearance and would have contacted him years ago, to disclose the details of the last night that I saw him."

"I thought that's why you came here in August. You said that you were going to make amends with someone from your past," Allison sniffled.

I was, and I did try to explain to him, but it was, as they say, too little too late. After he left, I met someone who taught me the true meaning of love. Love is respect, forgiveness, unselfishness... laughter, trust and mutual. After our conversation today, Hiram and I, well ... we're no longer in love with each other. Oh yes, Hiram loves you, this I am certain. But, he is not in love with you either, and I think you know that." Naomi pulled Allison closer, "Please Baby, life is so precious, don't waste a minute more waiting for dreams that have no basis in reality. I truly believe that if you live your life to the best of your abilities and trust in God, you will find that special person. At this very moment, he is somewhere, out there waiting for you. When you are both prepared for the relationship and the time is right, your paths will cross and you will soon recognize each other as soul mates. Meeting Hiram was an important part of the preparation for your future relationship with that person, tailored specifically for you. A wise man once, no twice, told me the most important thing you can have is, patience, my dear. Now, dry your eyes my sweet girl. Come with the faith that your life is in good hands." Naomi brushed the stray curls away from Allison's face and took her hand. "I would like you to meet that man, the man I was destined to be with. He should be arriving shortly."

Meanwhile, Hiram returned to the parlor, to find the Zigmanns entertaining the most recent visitor to the manor. The middle-aged gentleman turned mid-conversation, when silence encompassed the room with Master Hiram's entry. Hiram stood tall in the archway, squinting, questioning the familiarity of the red-bearded man, who sat reserved and unprepared for his nephew's worst possible reaction to his presence.

"Edward?" The only word spoken, gave cause for every member in the room to straighten in his or her seat with baited breath.

"Hello, Hiram," he answered, praying for his acceptance.

"You're alive, Edward!" As a condemned prisoner freed to live his life over, the ecstatic nephew maneuvered his way, through the seated Zigmanns, to properly greet his equally overjoyed uncle. The men embraced with unyielding warmth and forgiveness, sharing the rekindled flame of their lost relationship restored. The Zigmanns, familiar with the family history, found the sentimental scene tearing at their heartstrings.

"How can it be? I'm so relieved, so very happy to see you, Uncle Edward!" Hiram's instinctive reference to Edward as "uncle", immediately relaxed all those in attendance, and lit a spark of laughter, which quickly consumed the debilitating silence. The reunited men uncomfortably wiped the droplets that slipped from their eyes, then spoke briefly of the past and Edward's identity change, when all eyes darted to the hall, where Naomi appeared in the company of her solemn daughter.

"Naomi, Edward is alive!" Hiram announced.

"Yes, I know Hiram; it was a surprise to me, too." Naomi confirmed with an enamored smile, that Hiram understood immediately. Naomi proudly led her daughter across the room to introduce her to her soul mate, when the tiny pink sweater, which Eloise held in her lap, temporarily distracted her. Naomi directed a fleeting glance toward Hiram. The excitement of her daughter's introduction, dismissed any further thought of the sacred infant apparel, tucked in Amanda's small trunk, hidden away from the world, on the third floor.

"Edward, this is my beautiful daughter, Allison," Naomi's smile broadened when Edward reached for Allison's hand and gently placed a kiss upon it.

"Hello, Allison. This is a great pleasure. Your beautiful mother and I have been anxiously anticipating your arrival, and well... here you are... all together, I mean we're all together," he stumbled, as a flush of pink covered his cheeks, highlighting his bright red beard. Everyone laughed; Allison smiled and hugged "the wise man who quite obviously loved her mother dearly."

In the commotion, Hiram, feeling a tinge of discomfort in the family setting, moved close to Mr.

Zigmann and asked, "Would you mind driving me
to the village, Mr.Zigmann?"

"Not at all, sir," Albert obliged and excused
himself to hitch up the carriage. Hiram offered the
families the hospitality of his home, for as long as
they deemed necessary to become acquainted, and
shook his uncle's hand, followed by a nostalgic hug.
He affirmed that they would speak again in the
near future, while he casually retrieved his hat and
overcoat from the hall rack. He grasped the handle
of his suitcase, now splitting the pair of luggage,
which sat quietly together in the hall. Hiram briefly
studied the feminine carpetbag, left to fend for itself. He took a deep breath then turned to Eloise.

"You and your husband have done a marvelous job, caring for the estate. My thanks to both of
you."

Eloise nodded and thanked him for the compliment. Then with an encouraging smile and a
quick glance across the room to the infatuated,
young Guillaume, he addressed Allison, "I wish you
well, and beware of the many, young handsome
gentlemen, who will find you to be irresistible." Allison lowered her head, without making eye contact
with either man.

He turned to Naomi, "Thank you, Love, for
everything." Hiram then faced his uncle and re-
quested, "Edward, contact me, if you have any further trouble with Nathan and please take care of
these wonderful ladies." He closed the door to the
portal behind him, before Edward had a chance to
respond.

"I will, Hiram," Edward whispered. Naomi's
eyes saddened, as she stared blankly at the empty
hall, empathizing with a man who seemed to have

lost everyone important in his life. Her thoughts returned to the third floor, his mother's room and Hannah, Hiram's missing twin. Edward fearfully looked on, as Naomi and Allison stood despondent, over the absence of his nephew. However, a sigh of relief and his grateful smile returned, with the gleam that shone in Naomi's eyes, when he placed his arm about her.

The suave, debonair Guillaume, sensing the darkness surrounding Allison, flew from the window seat, without a second thought, for his final rescue attempt. Stumbling over the ottoman, sitting next to the sofa, he crashed to the floor, with all the grace of your average buffoon. The sound of the collision sent Eloise and Allison to their feet. Allison's sullen face gave way to an amused grin, ascending from her melancholy cloud of despair. Upon seeing the blushing white knight for the very first time, she reached to lend a helping hand, with a soft spoken "hello." Guillaume's bright smile was overshadowed by Hiram's unexpected return.

"I forgot something," the Master announced, glancing down with raised eyebrows at the flipped ottoman and its victim, sprawled on the floor. Spying the youthful hands, clutched in mid-air, he commented with a Cheshire smile, "Interesting approach, old man." Hiram set the ottoman upright, located the small wooden box on the parlor table, and then placed the treasure in his right coat pocket.

"Good day, ladies and gentlemen," he tipped his hat, bidding them farewell once again.

Hiram climbed into the cab of the aged, horse-drawn, carriage and closed the door behind him. He pulled the ornately carved box from his pocket and held it securely on his lap, as he took a final look at his remarkably rejuvenated home, Lochmoor's McDonnally Manor. His thoughts erratically raced, from the troubling encounters with the lovely mother and daughter, to the memory of the reuniting embrace with his uncle.

The carriage skipped, care freely through the hills, leaving the estate in the past, while Hiram, once again, fumbled nervously with the treasured box. He slowly lifted the lid, praying softly for the contents to miraculously reappear. The sparkle of serenity twinkled in his eyes, as he lifted the small tattered holy book from the box, with pious reverence.

The "faith" that his grandmother, Sarah, had warned him to protect, had been, sacredly restored and now a symphony of loving thoughts filled the coach, which delivered him, swiftly across the moors.

Hiram Geoffrey McDonnally sat back, clutching the book in his right hand, the box in his left. His beaming countenance, illuminated by the October sun, reflected a renewed life, as he rode peacefully to the village, with the promise of a wonderful future.

The Beginning

"So long Thy power has blest me,
sure it still
Will lead me on
O'er moor and fen,
O'er crag and torrent, till
The night is gone;
And with the morn those angel
faces smile
Which I have loved long since,
and lost awhile!"

— John Henry Newman

Non-fictional facts referenced in Patience, My Dear

Events:

Crimean War
 Zulu War
 World War I
Collapse of Tay Bridge
Suffragette demonstration
Assignment to Munich Opera
Australian meat in London
London Phone exchange
Theft of the Mona Lisa
Sinking of the Titanic
Invention of zipper and permanent wave
Cricket matches in Dover
Barnum and Bailey Circus in London
Introduction of Khaki Campbell ducks

People:

John Campbell
Irene and Vernon Castle
Emily Dickens
D.H. Lawrence
Jack London
Lachlan Macqaurie
Thomas Moore
Mrs. Pankhurst
Jack the Ripper

Acknowledgements

Crowl, Philip A. The Intelligent Traveller's Guide to Historic Scotland. New York: Congdon & Weed, Inc., 1986.

Discovery Channel. Scotland. Maspeth, New York: Langenscheidt Publishing Group, 2003.

Grun, Bernard. The Timetables of History: A Horizontal Linkage of People and Events. New York: Simon and Schuster, 1982.

Kightly, Charles. The Customs and Ceremonies of Britain: An Encyclopaedia of Living Traditions. New York: Thames and Hudson Inc., 1986.

Macgregor, Jimmie. Jimmie Macgregor's Scotland. London: BBC Books, 1993.

Palmer, Martin and Nigel Palmer. England, Scotland, Wales: The Guide To Sacred Sites and Pilgrim Routes in Britain. Mahwah, New Jersey: Paulist Press, 2000.

Visual Geography Series. Scotland in Pictures. Minneapolis: Learner Publications Company, 1991.

Webster's New Biographical Dictionary. Springfield: Merriam-Webster Inc, 1988.

Poetry Excerpts

Chapter I-*When Lilacs Last in the Dooryard Bloom*
 Walt Whitman

Chapter II-*Sonnet LXI*
William Shakespeare

Chapter III-*Perfect Woman*
William Wordsworth

Chapter IV-*Lord Ullin's Daughter*
Thomas Campbell

Chapter V-*Where There's A Will There's A Way.*
Eliza Cook

Chapter VI-*The Crooked Footpath*
Oliver Wendell Holmes

Chapter VII-*Somebody's Mother*
Mary Dow Brine

Chapter VIII-*A Psalm of Life*
Henry Wadsworth Longfellow

Chapter IX-*She Walks in Beauty*
Lord Byron

Chapter X-*Oh My Luve's Like a Red, Red Rose*
Robert Burns

Chapter XI-*Life's Mirror*
Madeline Bridges

Chapter XII-*In the Evil Days*
John Greenleaf Whittier

Lead, Kindly Light
John Henry Newman

A NOTE FROM THE AUTHOR:

*I am a firm believer
that education should be an ongoing endeavor.
I stand by the unwritten law
that education should be entertaining
for young and old alike.
Thus, I incorporate
historic places, people and events
in my novels
for your learning pleasure.*

*With loving thoughts,
Arianna Snow*

To order more copies of
Patience, My Dear
Visit the Golden Horse Ltd.
website :

www.ariannaghnovels.com

Watch for the sequel to
Patience, My Dear!

DISCARD